To all the wonderful Aunties

The Choice to Love Unconditionally

A Mirror Held Up With Love
Beth takes her chance to get out of town. Escaping a life that feels like an invisible trap.
But talking to her Great Auntie Lou makes Beth face herself.

Auntie to the Rescue
Beloved Auntie Claudia hears about a crisis from two sides. Rather than feeling caught in the middle, she treasures the chance to build a bridge.

When Simple Love Saves a Life
Bev answers a call for help from her sweet nephew Jody. Ready to offer support and love for whatever he faces. No matter how scary or strange the trouble.

Love that Spans the Generations
An emergency phone call sends Margaux flying to see her niece Chelsea.
But Chelsea's anxiety and fear about new motherhood threaten to drown her own joy.

The Cure for Homesickness
Soren's dream of riding his own airhorse awaits. As long as he manages his first time away from home. But his ongoing lack of sleep threatens everything.

Aunties Among Us:
Five Tales of Fabulous Women

Copyright © 2021 by Kari A. Kilgore

All rights reserved

Published 2021 by Spiral Publishing, Ltd.
www.SpiralPublishing.net
St. Paul, Virginia

Book and cover design copyright © 2021 by Spiral Publishing, Ltd.

Cover art copyright © 2021 by yupiramos | depositphotos.com

ISBN-13: 978-1-63992-018-1
Large Print ISBN-13: 978-1-63992-019-8
Hardcover ISBN-13: 978-1-63992-020-4

Additional copyright information for previously published material at the back of the book.

AUNTIES AMONG US

FIVE TALES OF FABULOUS WOMEN

KARI KILGORE

SPIRAL PUBLISHING, LTD.

CONTENTS

INTRODUCTION

Even when I was growing up, I never especially wanted to have children of my own.

I didn't dislike the idea, exactly, or think I'd be bad at it or anything like that. My childhood was fairly typical for a free-range kid raised in the 1970s and 1980s, so I wasn't trying to avoid passing along some kind of trauma.

I simply didn't wish or hope or even daydream about being a birth mother or raising children full-time.

What I did think about sometimes was how cool it would be to be a *grandparent*.

Getting to take kids for short stretches of time, and go out and do fun things with them. Attend plays or games or birthday parties, without having to do all the driving back and forth on a daily basis, or endless baking for bake sales, or sitting through PTA meetings.

Then going home or sending them back home most of the time, so they and I would be happy and comfortable at the end of the day.

I remember wishing I could do all of that without having to be a parent first.

I didn't realize until I was into my thirties that lucky aunties have that exact job description.

Let me back up a step and define my terms a bit, because not everyone uses them the same way.

I'm using *auntie* as a slightly different role and relationship than aunt. Yes, they're both generally adult women. And they can both have nieces and nephews.

But for my purposes here and for the stories in *Aunties Among Us*, aunties aren't raising their own kids, as in biological children. They may be happily child-free like me, or they may have wanted or still plan to have children of their own. They may have raised their kids in the previous generation.

And they may not even be technically related to the children they have an auntie relationship with. Most of the kids I've been close to over the years have been the ones I love by choice.

The most important thing is that unique relationship. The vital role of a special adult in a child's life who can focus exclusively on them during visits or outings. With no worries about their own children, while the kids aren't worried about cousins or siblings to take up the auntie's attention.

Of course men can fill this role, and often do. My husband Jason A. Adams has proudly served as Red-Headed Jason and Unka J to the kids in our lives for years.

Auntie was the role I wanted to play in a child's life, even while I still *was* a kid.

I was incredibly lucky to have that wonderful relationship with my godmother Virginia and her sister Victoria, women of my grandparents' generation who didn't have children of their own. The time I spent with them seemed magical to me.

I was away from other kids, and not expected to be still and quiet like I was in school.

These two women—educated and independent and

accomplished in ways most of the women their age in my family didn't have the opportunity to be—never talked down to me or treated me like a child.

They talked to me like a *person*, with ideas and preferences and opinions of my own.

Partly because they didn't have other kids my age who quite reasonably needed their attention, they were able to relate to me in ways my parents, aunts and uncles, and even my grandparents often couldn't.

It was absolutely wonderful!

So when my cousins started having children of their own, I was determined to fill that role in their lives as much as I possibly could. And of course when my two nephews came along years later, I was overjoyed when one of them dubbed me Auntie Moon.

They've recently shortened that to Moon as they approach the wilds of their teenage years, which I find both adorable and hilarious.

I expect them to call me some variation of Auntie Moon at least until they turn thirty, then we'll negotiate.

Just like with all my auntie kids, I get to hear things they'd never tell their parents, and answer questions they'd never ask adults with kids of their own. So far, nothing has crossed the line into dangerous or worrisome, and I'd let their parents know if it did.

What I mainly get is a delightful glimpse into their brilliant imaginations and developing minds. Not to mention a clear insight into how their generation sees the world, and how culture, entertainment, and technology are shifting along with them.

All that and I have an excellent excuse to get out and do silly and fun stuff with them!

Being both an auntie and an aunt has let me welcome an incredible group of kids and now young adults into my life. I hope I've taught them a thing or two, but I know I can't teach them nearly as much as they've taught me.

When I decided to write a collection of stories about my fellow aunties, I wanted to include a variety of women in that loving, mentoring role. And since I've been fortunate enough to spend precious time with quite the range of young people, writing about all kinds of kids and even adults was a natural.

So I conjured a lovely crew of aunties and auntie kids to help me tell these stories. I hope you enjoy spending time with them as much as I did.

Patience, and Perspective introduces you to a woman who has chosen to share her life with her best friend's children. As is so often the case, that commitment doesn't end when the child leaves diapers and grade school events and getting ready for bake sales behind. Claudia gets drawn into an all-too-common young adult drama, and has to figure out how to support two generations through a challenging day.

One of the wonderful side effects of being part of the lives of several different children, and over more than one generation, is aunties often pick up an extensive array of kid-care skills. In *Sweet Calm Before the Family Storm*, Auntie Go knows more than enough to help her grown niece ease into the shocking reality of sudden parenthood. And gets some wonderful baby-cuddling time in the process.

Sometimes aunties are the ones a troubled young person turns to when they're afraid to go anywhere else, no matter how badly they need someone to talk to. In *One Simple Word*, Bev has a chance to show just how the unconditional and honest love of an auntie can make a difference to a kid who needs it most.

A good auntie is often a great-aunt, and the kids she cares for never quite outgrow needing her friendship and support. *In A Gentle Nudge in the Right Direction*, a prequel story in my Voices Through Time universe, Beth Azen turns to a beloved and trusted great-auntie during a challenging time in her life. When it comes to matters of the heart, our aunties somehow seem to know us better than we know ourselves.

The Foundation of His Past visits the epic fantasy world of my Misfortune and Magic series, and proves that even kids who live with magic every day still need their aunties. In this case, Tante Fodry is a professional auntie to young airhorse rider trainees. Possibly because she's helped many of them through the difficult transition of moving away from home, she manages to find the perfect loving touch when one of them struggles to sleep through the night.

All the stories in this collection focus on people of various ages turning to their aunties for help during upsetting times. While this is absolutely a vital part of these relationships that so often deepen into friendships over time, in real life that foundation of trust is built on much happier times spent together.

And yes, of course, drama makes for better storytelling.

I hope you've enjoyed these peeks into the bonds between aunties and the ones they share their gifts of love and support with as much as I've enjoyed writing them.

Whether you're an auntie (or uncle) yourself, or you have memories of that special grownup in your life, or both, my wish is that these stories leave you with an appreciation for how much these relationships can change everyone involved. Hopefully for the better.

Exactly like my aunties and my auntie kids have for me.

I've often written about special aunties, so if you'd like to spend story time with more of them, check out www. KariKilgore.com/Aunties.

If you're looking for more stories where speculative elements are slight or not there at all, pay a visit to www.KariKilgore.com/ContemporaryFiction.

Introduction

You'll discover more fantasy of many kinds at www.KariKilgore.com/Fantasy.

For more visits to the Appalachian Mountains in and around Virginia, head on over to www.KariKilgore.com/TalesfromAppalachia.

You can also check out www.KariKilgore.com to learn more about me and find other short stories, along with novellas, novels, and more collections.

If you want to keep up with what I'm doing next, get free stories, read exclusive content not available anywhere else, and see adorable pet photos, head over to The Confidential Adventure Club at www.ConfidentialAdventureClub.com. Hope to see you there!

And last but certainly not least, thank you for your support of me and my writing. It means the world to me and keeps me coming back to tell the next tale.

KARI KILGORE

AUTHOR OF THE WORRY TRAP AND A RACE AGAINST TEA TIME

Patience, and Perspective

For every Mamma blessed with a co-Mamma

PATIENCE, AND PERSPECTIVE

MOST OF THE TIME, Claudia Bell loved her job.

Sure, keeping the IT department running more or less smoothly for a good-sized Atlanta law firm could get hectic. New associates needed a lot of hand-holding, and a surprising amount of training to get up to speed on all the systems and reporting. Long-time partners somehow managed to need almost as much help, but not because they'd been dragging their brains through law school for the last few years.

With a few of them, the problem was more they preferred the days when someone else handled all the pesky computer stuff *for* them.

Then came the challenges of keeping a crew of help desk folks happy and organized, even in the face of fielding all the questions from the associates. And occasionally near-abuse from people who'd been at the firm long enough to know better.

Add in wrangling the deskside support people who *didn't* have the advantage of not having to deal with partners, associates, legal secretaries, paralegals, and everyone else face-to-face.

The challenge of putting all of that together and making it work was the kind of giant, ongoing, ever-changing puzzle that Claudia delighted in solving.

Even on a day like this, attending a conference with other law firm IT managers usually brought a fascinating new set of hints and skills to add to her collection.

And anyway, the food at these big events was free, plentiful, and often pretty dang tasty.

Right now she sat in a swanky Midtown Atlanta hotel ballroom, all crystal chandeliers and green velvet curtains and chairs with plush cushions. The kind designed for real humans, with backsides and legs and all, rather than for an as-of-yet undiscovered species of square-assed creature that enjoyed sitting on sharp, angular plastic for hours on end.

The room was pleasantly cool but not deep-freeze, a lovely contrast to the sweltering July morning. Claudia had arrived prepared after years of experience—packing a sweater, a scarf, and a lap blanket in her bag, fully expecting to need them all. Instead she and her fellow attendees all sat comfortably in their usual variety of never-quite-fashionable attire.

Everything from golf shirts and khakis to jeans and t-shirts to dresses and jackets, depending on how uptight their particular firm happened to be.

Whoever arranged this conference hadn't skimped on food or drinks, either. Each place at the rows of tables draped in white cotton with burgundy skirts all around was set with a water glass and pitchers full of ice water at the ready, as usual. But they'd also included a smaller juice glass and a heavy white coffee mug at each spot.

Luxury for a group accustomed to fending for themselves with refillable water bottles and travel mugs, all of dubious cleanliness.

The heavenly aroma of freshly brewed coffee and tea drifted through the air, along with hints of equally fresh orange juice. A massive spread along one wall offered all kinds of bagels, muffins, doughnuts, and the most decadent selection of danishes Claudia had ever seen at a conference.

Not one of them baked before that same morning unless she missed her very educated guess.

She'd already knocked back several cups of excellent coffee and devoured an everything bagel with onion-and-chive cream cheese. Now she was greedily eyeing a raspberry danish despite her normally light morning eating habits.

Because she needed a base for the coffee she would need to keep consuming to get through the current presentation about a new database administration system. One not suited for her firm in any possible way.

Making this one of the rare times Claudia actively *dis*liked her job.

So when her watch buzzed with a text message notification, she jerked her arm under the table so fast she nearly upended her condensation-covered glass of water. At least it would have fallen away from her laptop, though toward it would have given her an excuse to get the hell out of there.

She smiled when she saw the message was from Lanie, daughter of her best college friend Sharon, and the closest thing Claudia had to a child of her own.

But a frown gradually took over her face as she read.

Hey Auntie C

Fair warning, incoming from Mom. All bad, all about me.

Got a minute to talk?

Love, L

"Oh, poor kid," Claudia whispered, shaking her head.

She and Sharon had met during freshman year and hit it off immediately. Same oddball sense of humor, same interest in tech, same stubborn determination to succeed in a field that was hardly easy for women back in the 1990s.

They'd supported each other through hookups and breakups, all-night parties and study sessions alike.

Served as maids of honor at each other's weddings, and mourned and celebrated a dozen milestones along the way. Through Sharon's three kids with her perfectly matched husband Keith, and Claudia's thankfully low-key divorce and intense but far happier second marriage.

Claudia loved all of Sharon's kids, but so many things about Lanie made their relationship extra-special.

She slipped her phone out from under an untouched leatherbound notebook—thoughtfully provided by the conference organizers, and sure to make someone a lovely gift. A quick glance to make sure the people seated around her were in fact paying close attention to the front of the room, and she was back under the table and tapping.

Of course I can talk, you'd be doing me a favor!

No word yet, what should I be bracing for?

Love, Auntie C

She'd just hit send with another message popped in.

The promised incoming from Sharon.

SOS to co-Mamma, trouble for our girl! Begging me to let her tell you, but losing my grip.

Help!

That was all Claudia needed to see. She wasn't the least bit sad to slip her laptop into her backpack and lean toward her assistant, who was somehow entirely caught up in the presentation. Hopefully not with thoughts of trying to convince Claudia they should consider adopting a new system they absolutely did not need.

Sadly, since Jenny was as eager and excitable and susceptible to buying into The Next Big Thing as anyone newly entering the world of IT, days spent fending off those suggestions were a near-certainty.

Claudia mouthed *Gotta take this* as she stood, then scooted out the heavy door at the back of the room.

Before she could decide whether to call Sharon or Lanie, Lanie rang through.

"What's up, Lanie?"

A long, rumbling sigh had Claudia bracing herself for the worst, whatever that might turn out to be for a dramatic twenty-three-year-old. Lanie's tense voice and rushed words made it clear how far up the scale of upset she'd already gone.

"I'm soooo sorry to bother you at work, but, well, anyway. Work is not my favorite thing right now, or I guess I should say lack of work. I got fired today, Auntie C."

Claudia bit back something like "From a job that was never going to suit you in the first place?" or "So you're not sick or hurt or in physical danger?" and parked herself and her backpack on a huge, artfully exaggerated purple sofa just down the hall from the conference room. The extra-tall back and curved seats would have fit right in at a modern art museum.

All the other conference room doors were closed, and the hall was dim and whisper-quiet, not to mention edging past cool and into the deep-freeze. The only people moving along the colorful geometric carpet under tasteful hidden lighting were white-jacketed restaurant employees setting up an early lunch buffet for some other group.

"Oh Lanie honey, I'm sorry. What happened?"

"Please don't tell Mom this, but it was pretty much my fault. I messed up a big order for invitations for my manager's boss, some kind of major fundraiser they're really depending on. I got the date wrong. Can you believe that?"

"I can't believe they're still sending out paper invitations. Too late to order new ones?"

"Right? Who does that more than fifteen years into the twenty-first century, especially for fifteen hundred people! Yeah, they're ordering new ones. But my manager said something along the lines of how they could have paid my salary, or they could pay for a new print run. Which I know is bullshit since I *ordered* them, but I just didn't feel up to the argument after that. Which is probably just what she wanted when she said it."

Claudia was glad Lanie couldn't see her face just then. Her inexperienced and terribly distraught self probably wouldn't have taken a nostalgic smile very well.

Because Claudia had more of what felt like early-career disasters stored up in her memory banks than she wanted to admit to anyone.

Even someone who needed comforting.

"Listen, we all make mistakes," she said. "It really is part of the program early in your working life. You just get your resume back out there and you'll find something. One mix-up doesn't knock out your degrees or portfolio or experience. Hell, you'll probably find something that suits you a lot better, and fast."

"That's what I think, and what I told Mom. They really did have me doing stuff I could have handled in high school, and no real path forward. But you know how she is. Wouldn't slow down the stream of advice about how I could have *not* done the thing long enough to *listen* to me. Well, I already *did* the thing, and I'm upset enough about it. Maybe she could let me try to fix it, you know?"

Claudia leaned back against the sofa's absurdly high back and sighed.

She did know. Wonderful as Sharon was, she never had quite outgrown her youthful ability to get herself wound up even more than Lanie was, probably more so. Claudia knew

Sharon—and Lanie—would eventually regain a glide state. Decades of experience taught her that.

But the two of them could play off of each other in ways that kept them both spun up for an amazingly long time.

And she and Sharon's husband and even the rowdy twin boys who had so quickly followed Lanie all knew the best thing to do when Sharon and Lanie got locked into their mutual escalations was to stay out of the way.

Or, sometimes, if Claudia could find the right timing and angle, she'd manage to divert one or both of them into calmer airspace.

"Okay, then get started fixing the thing now is what I say. Where are you, hon? At your apartment, or at Sharon and Keith's office?"

Lanie laughed, and thankfully a good bit of the tension had left her voice when she spoke again.

"I just walked in the door at home. No way in hell I'm going over to Mom and Dad's office right now. That's just what I need. A Sharon Abrams-Gregg Special Production of *Another Thousand and One Ways Lanie Could Have Not Screwed Up*. Followed immediately by *Twice as Many Ways to Avoid This Problem in the Future*, and *An Entire Encyclopedia of How to Get Your Life Back on Track*. All while Mr. Keith Gregg waits on standby for when she finally takes a breath so he can finally offer the required Dad list of how everything really is going to be okay."

An intense flashback hit Claudia just then, of the frantic first few weeks after Sharon realized she was pregnant again, long before the planned target of Lanie going to pre-school. Lanie hadn't even turned one when Sharon got the happy-stressful-wonderful-shocking news.

She'd spent a whole lot of time saying almost the exact same kinds of things Lanie was saying now. Claudia knew for a fact Keith had gotten his amazing stock of reassurances started during those whiplash days as well. For himself and for Sharon.

Sharon's self-induced and thankfully short-lived temporary tailspin was part of accepting the massive upcoming change in her life, sure. And a way to admit to herself, her husband, and her best friend that she was in way, way over her head.

Claudia's habit of spending extra time with Lanie started not long after, one everyone still appreciated all these years later.

"You have a point about not getting in your mom's face right now. How about we grab lunch and talk about your next steps? Get started on finding the next thing?"

Claudia's phone buzzed in her ear, and she didn't have to look to know who was calling.

Lanie was equally certain.

"That's Mom ringing through, isn't it? She promised to let me tell you, but I knew she wouldn't be able to hold out long."

"You gonna hate me if I point out that she *did* let you tell me?"

Lanie snorted, and Claudia saw her bright and vivid in her mind, shaking her head hard enough that her brown ringlets danced around her head.

"'Course I'm not going to hate you. Like she always says, you were hers first. But if you don't call her right back, she'll get even more of a boil going in her kettle."

"You have a point, and a unique way of saying it, as you so often do. Let me talk to her and see how she's doing. Then I really would love to duck out of this conference early and meet you for lunch. They won't be getting to anything I need to be here for until this afternoon. My treat, since you've gotten yourself newly unemployed and all. Sound good?"

"Like you'd ever let me pay for lunch, Auntie C. Good luck avoiding the drama on your next call. You'll need it."

Claudia rolled her eyes at the thought of this sweet child thinking she could give advice about talking Sharon down from her anxiety whirlwind. A dance Claudia been lovingly engaging in with Sharon for a solid decade before Lanie was born, and now just as lovingly did with a new generation.

Even if that new generation wouldn't admit the similarities just yet, if ever.

"I'll do my best, kid. Go sit still for a minute, take a deep breath. Then text me your favorite hot new Midtown lunch spot and grab us a reservation if it needs one. Talk to you soon."

Claudia closed her eyes for a few seconds before dialing in to the next tidal wave of emotion. Honestly, neither Sharon nor Lanie were that bad, even when they got upset. Quite a few members of Claudia's family and her former in-laws made the two of them look like ripples in a pond compared to the tempests that crowd could whip up over the least little thing.

That was one reason she was glad the in-laws were former, and that she rarely saw her own relatives who so clearly enjoyed the constant undercurrent of spats and infighting and all-out fights.

Much as she didn't miss those parts of her life, she would miss the excitement of Sharon and Lanie. They let her enjoy the involvement without dragging her into the uncomfortable middle.

And she dearly loved both of them for it.

She hit the return call button rather than listening to the message, since Sharon would repeat the whole thing anyway.

"She told you?" Sharon said, with an exasperated rush to her words that echoed Lanie's quite nicely. "What a rotten *stinking* day for our girl. That jerk she works for—or she *did* work for—didn't deserve anyone as talented as Lanie in that half-assed excuse for a job."

Claudia was once again grateful to have the cover of a phone conversation to hide her grin. That was exactly the response she'd expected, and one Lanie never would have believed in a thousand years.

Sharon had two very different parent modes, like most parents did.

Concerned *for* the child, versus angry about what happened *to* the child.

And the difference between the two was impossible to imagine for an upset kid right in the thick of it all. Claudia had certainly been no exception at the same age with her own parents.

"She told me," Claudia said. "I don't think she's quite worked through feeling bad so she can get to feeling relieved, but she'll get there. Lanie's got way too many in-demand skills and experiences to worry about finding something else once she calms down."

"You *bet* she does. Of course she does, with me pushing her and you encouraging her all these years to get herself prepared. And her father too, of course." Now Claudia saw Sharon bright and clear in her mind's eye, running one hand through her own brown curls now touched with silver. "They were damn lucky to have someone of Lanie's caliber there to begin with. Some *smart* firm will thank their lucky stars and grab her. I tried to tell her that when she got the offer on this job, but she... Well, you know."

Claudia laughed, and a quick second later Sharon joined in. No chance at all they weren't both remembering a dozen equally awful or even worse situations when they were the same age.

"You mean she listened to you about as well as either of us listened to our parents back then, or to anyone more than a couple of years older than us? Or maybe that she has to make her own mistakes to get the lessons through her rock-solid wall of smart and stubborn and determined-to-be-independent? Nope, never heard of such a thing in my whole life."

"You are evil and wretched, Claudia, just like you have been most of my life. And I don't want to imagine what any of us would do without you. I know you've got that conference thing going, since I managed to weasel myself out of the same one. Guessing you made plans to get Lanie out of her apartment and out of her head anyway?"

"You bet, and you were entirely right about the conference, at least so far. Lanie's doing me a favor by giving me an excuse to skip out until later. We're going to lunch as soon as she picks the spot, since she knows all the hot new places I'm too old and busy and out of touch to keep up with anymore. Should I ask her for advice for when I'll need to get you out of *your* office and out of *your* head?"

Sharon blew a remarkably fart-like raspberry into the phone, a reaction that still set both of them giggling even well into their fifties.

"Speak for yourself, old lady. But...on second thought, you might want to ask Lanie to suggest a suitably *mature* dinner idea for you and me. That way all three of our rowdy smelly boys can enjoy a night in, so they can burp and fart and scratch and tell stupid jokes to their hearts' content. I'm sure Keith has a few titles left in his collection of the worst movies ever made to spoil our sons' impressionable minds with."

Claudia looked up at the *thunks* of several conference room doors opening at once. Sure enough, a flood of sleepy or irritated or excited computer-centric humanity came pouring out. All of them focused on moving fast enough to shed some of that wonderful caffeine and hustle back in time to grab a handful of yummy free carbohydrates before it was all gone.

The aroma of the other group's ridiculously early lunch buffet wafting through the air was sure to intensify that effect greatly.

Claudia raised her voice over the sudden jump in wonderfully geeky conversation.

"I'll ask Lanie what she'd suggest without letting her know who I'll be dining with, not that she hasn't already got us figured out. Every bit as much as the boys have got both of us and Keith mapped out and dancing on their sweet little strings. The inmates just got sprung from the asylum for a bio-break, so I better get moving before I get trampled."

"Okay, sweetie, get yourself away from the nerd stampede. I'm sorry you're missing a bunch of the conference dealing with all our drama. You know I appreciate you more than coffee, right? Every one of us does."

Claudia snorted, watching her bright-eyed young assistant glance around the throng, spot her, and charge forward unswerving through the masses, conference-swag leather notebook clutched against her chest like a holy stone tablet brought down from on high.

"I'm calling bullshit about the coffee, but right back at you, hon. You know as well as I do Lanie feels the same way about you, even when she's too much *like* you to say it. No worries about the conference. I've got my own excruciatingly detailed re-cap on the way, and I'll have that much and more after lunch this afternoon. You remember my assistant Jenny, right? About Lanie's age, and just as convinced she's got the job and the industry and the whole damn world figured out?"

"Whew, have fun with *that*, Auntie C. Sounds like you got a good one there. Taking notes for the boss will be good for her, and slowing down enough to actually listen to her will be good for you, right? Anyway, give our Lanie a hug that she doesn't know comes from me. I'll give her one myself once we both calm down."

The phone buzzed as Claudia ended the call, and she had just enough time for a quick glance before she had to confront All the Glories of a Database We'll Never Need.

Meet me in twenty. Great new place, trendy and geeky, you'll love it.

I'll be fine with Mom, not that you don't already know that.
Can't wait to plot and scheme with you!

Claudia glanced at the restaurant name and address, tapped a quick hand-blowing-kiss emoji, and put the phone away, bracing herself for the oncoming storm surge of enthusiasm.

Not for the first time, or the last, Sharon was right.

Maybe Claudia *would* learn something new and interesting from taking the time to listen to Jenny, even if it wasn't about databases. And she'd get a beautifully detailed set of notes to go with a more confident and prepared assistant to boot.

Amazing how often her Auntie C experience carried over into the rest of her life.

Or maybe it was the other way around.

Either way, she greeted Jenny with true curiosity and an honest smile.

"Thank goodness you're here, Jenny. I've got to duck out for a couple of hours. Take your usual fantastic notes, and we'll get together for lunch tomorrow to go over it all. I just heard about this fantastic new place I know you're going to love."

KARI KILGORE

AUTHOR OF THE WORRY TRAP AND SONGS IN THE MOUNTAIN

Sweet Calm Before the Family Storm

For everyone who takes the time to comfort a new parent

SWEET CALM BEFORE THE FAMILY STORM

MARGAUX ROBBINS MAY HAVE HAD sweeter bursts of nostalgia in her fifty-three years, but she couldn't bring one to mind just yet.

The sprawling old farmhouse at the end of a bumpy gravel road explained part of it. Hidden far back in the woods of eastern Michigan, the turn-of-the-twentieth-century beauty had Victorian decorative touches to go with solid and practical Midwestern construction.

The current vibrant gold paint job set the house off nicely against a thick stand of oaks and pines all dressed up in lush, late summertime greenery. Deep autumn-blue-sky accents brought out the woodwork twists and curlicues tucked into all the eaves, porch railings, and window frames.

Someone had a fire going nearby, possibly for an early campsite supper. Margaux caught herself wishing for the steaks, potatoes, and corn her grandfather used to grill when she was a kid, and the rich, buttery biscuits her grandmother baked to perfection.

She'd indulged for years before she'd ever imagined giving

up red meat in her twenties, or having a doctor tell her how that decision cast a favorable echo all the way into her middle-aged bloodwork.

She'd just settled herself onto a second-level porch overlooking a little pond edged by feathery grass and brown-tipped cattails. The tranquil view was worth the humidity and lingering heat of a September day.

After hours spent crowded on a flight from Atlanta that morning, she welcomed the comfort of a curvy rocking chair that had to be almost as old as the house.

She'd sewn the cinnamon-brown cushions herself sometime in the early 2000s, during her own time living in the family homestead almost twenty years ago. The glorious couple of years spent here let her get her head and heart cleared from a heartbreaking divorce, and convinced her to go back to school in her late thirties. Her challenging career in graphic design had been worth every second of stress and worry and feeling weird about having homework again.

That career change and move down south reinvigorated her love life, too, resulting in a much happier marriage the second time around.

Everyone in the Robbins clan seemed to land here at one time or another, often in the middle of a big life transition. So the arrival of Margaux's youngest niece Chelsea McGill the day before was hardly a surprise.

Chelsea's announcement that she'd be bringing her newly adopted daughter toed the line somewhere between surprise and utter shocker. Especially since neither Margaux nor anyone else knew a baby was in the cards at all for Chelsea and her wife Regina.

Turns out they'd been trying to adopt for a while, and fear of yet another attempt falling through led them to keep all the news to themselves. And because life generally worked out that way, Jade's adoption came through much faster than expected.

Right now Chelsea leaned against the porch rail, arms crossed and too-thin face pale and drawn with stress. Her normally bouncy red hair hung dull and disorganized, and she'd traded in her typical stylish wardrobe for black sweatpants and a pink t-shirt a couple of sizes too big.

She'd deposited Jade in Margaux's lap only a few seconds before, letting out a sigh full of relief mixed with exhaustion.

And immediately started fretting about letting go of the baby at all.

"If Jade's too twitchy for you, Auntie Go, I'll take her back. She can be a real handful when she's squirmy."

Margaux smiled at the nickname all her nieces and nephews had used for her since the first one was born when she was barely out of high school. She'd welcomed the tradition continuing into her crop of great-nieces and nephews as much as hearing Chelsea use it again for the first time in years.

For her part, Jade had already squeezed her big blue eyes closed, with one tiny fist clutching Margaux's index finger in a viselike grip. She was about as far from twitchy as a gorgeous six-week-old could possibly be.

Her impossibly cute daisy-and-bumble-bee onesie only accelerated the instant falling-in-love effect.

"This precious little darling is nowhere near a handful just yet," Margaux said, her voice not much above a whisper. "And I'm about to float away on a river of nostalgia myself. Did you know I held you on this very porch when you were about the same age? Most of your cousins, too. Don't tell any of the others, but you were the easiest baby of all. At least so far. You might have competition now."

Chelsea leaned forward, pushing her hair behind her ears

and gazing at Jade. A ghost of a smile danced across her weary face.

"I hope you're willing to tell Regina that when she gets here. She's pretty much convinced I'm the most restless sleeper to ever draw breath. I might actually fulfill the title now that we've got Ms. Jade to take care of."

Margaux planted a delicate kiss on the fuzz of blonde hair on Jade's sweet-smelling head.

Chelsea's wife Regina had gotten caught up in a last-minute pre-sabbatical work emergency, combined with thunderstorms closing down the airports in St. Louis. Delaying their planned several-months-long retreat to the Michigan farmhouse by a day or two might not seem like much to an outside observer.

But to Chelsea—an only child with precious little experience caring for a baby—the hours apparently stretched out nearly to eternity.

"She'll be here before you know it," Margaux said. "You and Jade are going to be just fine."

Chelsea opened her mouth, then blinked and closed it with a huge sigh.

"I hadn't even *started* learning what to do," she finally said, "not that I could have soaked up everything I need to know in the couple of days before we left. From what everyone says, it was a pure miracle that Jade slept so much on our flight. That might have been the whole run on my new parent luck, huh?"

"Oh, I don't know," Margaux said, managing to tear her gaze away from Jade long enough to meet Chelsea's eyes. "I'd say we were both pretty lucky I was able to get such a quick flight out. I may not have raised a kid of my own, but I've spent more than enough time with them to know the ropes. Another thing that's not one bit luck is how calm and clean and happy this baby is, even after all the stress and nonsense of flying. Most adults don't get off a plane without wanting to sit down and cry, and looking like it. You're doing something right."

Then tears welling in Chelsea's eyes had Margaux wishing she was still little enough to pick up and hug, even though that would be quite a trick with a baby already sound asleep on her lap.

She waited several seconds, watching Chelsea blink and shake her head, hoping words would make it out. When Chelsea managed to let out a watery laugh and threw both hands up, Margaux took that as her signal to at least make the offer to help.

The fact that Chelsea managed to stay where she was instead of retrieving Jade had to be a good sign, even with her new-parent nervousness flaring up.

"You know you don't have to tell me anything you don't want to," Margaux said. "Same as it's been between us since you weren't much bigger than this sweetheart. So I'll just ask if you want to tell me what's got you so upset."

Thank goodness and years of honest conversations that Chelsea smiled when she spoke.

"You mean so I can dump all my emotional bullshit on you, same way I handed the kid over first chance I got?"

Margaux shifted Jade the tiniest little bit, tucking her more securely in one arm, then held out a hand to Chelsea. As she had since she was a giggling little girl, Chelsea offered her own hand for a quick Auntie Go kiss.

"I suppose you could say you handed this adorable little girl over," Margaux said, giving the back of Chelsea's hand a good smooch before she let go and again cradled Jade. "But we both know I wouldn't have lasted more than another fifteen or twenty seconds before I grabbed her up for a good hug. You know every bit as well that I'm here if you want to talk, judgement-free."

She didn't say what she was thinking, something along the lines of "If you didn't want my help, and if everything is totally fine, what was up with that late-night emergency phone call?"

Chelsea shook herself, and pulled her hair back into a quick knot at the back of her head. All at once, she looked a lot more like the confident, sassy young woman Margaux knew so well.

But she didn't miss the purplish bruises under Chelsea's lovely green eyes.

"I don't know how to say any of this without sounding awful and ungrateful and selfish," Chelsea began, before she caught sight of Margaux's raised eyebrow. "I know, I know, you said no judgement and you meant it, like you always have. Okay."

She closed her eyes and held her breath for a second before blurting out a flood of words that tumbled over themselves trying to get out.

"I'm afraid I'm so far in over my head with all of this that I can't even see the surface or where the fresh air is or a place where I might know what to do. And not just when she cries or coughs or spits up, but all the time. *All the time.* I have no idea what I'm doing and I'm scared to death every single second that I'm going to make a terrible mistake."

Chelsea's eyes flew open, and she drew in a great, gasping breath and wrapped her arms around herself in a panicky hug.

And now Margaux was the one with tears threatening to spill over and land on little Jade's precious, perfect face.

"Oh honey. I know this is hard to hear and harder to believe right now, but you're going to figure it all out. Plenty of people who love you will do everything we can to help. I promise. Speaking of people who love you, how's Regina doing?"

Chelsea slowly slid her hands down her arms until she clasped one in the other, staring down at her wedding ring. Margaux remembered the moment she and Regina exchanged those beautiful rings—each a twist of silver and black gold that held a gorgeous gemstone in a spiral setting. Ruby for Chelsea, and sapphire for Regina.

Margaux had been standing by Chelsea's side that day, and Chelsea's soft, romantic smile looked the same as it did right now.

"Regina is...the happiest I've ever seen her. She hasn't said it out loud, but I know she was born for this. Being a mother, taking care of a baby. Raising the next generation and all that was meant to be for her. I swear she's glowing, as if she's the one who had Jade, you know?"

When she looked up, the smile faded and an anxious frown took its place.

"I'm not sure *I* was meant to do any of this, though. Regina just seems to know every little thing before Jade even needs it, before she makes a sound. And I'm trying to re-learn all the parenting books and notes and videos that we watched for the last few years while we filled out adoption paperwork over and over again."

She stepped forward and brushed Jade's tiny hand where it gripped Margaux's finger. Chelsea's fingers trembled, but her smile held the same warmth and fierce love as on her wedding day.

"Then something happens, because of course that's how kids are," Chelsea went on, her voice thick with tears. "Jade so much as hiccups, and I panic, and I can't remember a single thing I read or heard or asked or learned. I'm just this clueless dork, lovestruck but useless when it comes to taking care of her. I somehow doubt this will be the only time I'm the mother-in-charge. I can't always depend on Regina to take over. That's not fair and I don't want to be that way. But I wouldn't leave a *goldfish* with someone as bad at this as I am."

Margaux held her own breath as Jade's body tensed, ready to shift her to a more comfortable position if she cried, or pat her back so she could burp, or simply hold her close and sing a nonsense lullaby until she settled down again.

Jade stretched her arms out, grunted a couple of times, and relaxed.

"One thing I want to point out," Margaux said, "then I'm going to ask you a question you can ignore if you want. *Regina* obviously trusts you with Jade, and I'd say that's who matters most. Now, did she have brothers and sisters?"

Chelsea laughed out loud, then covered her mouth in a hurry when Jade scowled.

"You know she did, you were at our wedding. Three brothers and two sisters. She's Auntie Reg about a dozen times over." She paused for a few seconds, rolled her eyes, and smiled. "And that's exactly what you were wanting me to say out loud, huh?"

Margaux shrugged one shoulder, adding a wink for good measure.

"You'll never catch me saying being an excellent auntie means you *must* have kids of your own, or even that you should want to. I'd be about nine different kinds of hypocrite if I said that. But I'm willing to guess that gave Auntie Reg a certain level of confidence when it comes to taking on a miniature human being full-time. You might need a breath or two to catch up is all. What does your mom say?"

Chelsea breathed in long and slow, standing up tall and drawing her shoulders back. Finally starting to look almost like her normal self, just with a clear lack of sleep and unusually casual wardrobe.

Pretty much like any shell-shocked brand-new parent, in other words.

"You know how Mom is. After she finishes interrogating me about every single thing we're doing and why and every one of Jade's vital statistics, she breezily tells me it will all work out. She did mention how much a baby disrupts your schedule, along with another in her vast collection of stories of how I kept her awake for approximately eighteen years."

She stepped forward and sat on the little wooden table beside Margaux's rocking chair, staring at Jade with an expression of pure adoration.

"Yeah, that sounds exactly like her," Margaux said. "I think she might be right about that last part, even if she's exaggerated the timeline a wee bit. You know I love your mother dearly, but she's still my bratty little sister. So I feel free to say she's giving you advice from the comfortable distance of a grandmother rather than as the exhausted and confused new mother I remember her being. This is a several-times-over great-aunt speaking, of course, so I'm operating from a solid basis of experience myself."

"What you're saying is Mom wasn't always the ultimate expert on all things baby that she makes herself sound like now? Next you'll be telling me she took every scrap of Grandmama's advice without ever arguing a word of it."

This time Margaux covered her own mouth to keep a too-loud-for-baby laugh from barking its way out into the tranquil afternoon.

Chelsea's honest and relaxed grin was a joy to behold.

"Oh *sure*, your mom never argued, or resisted, or just grabbed you up and walked out the door instead of talking about it one single second longer. We'll have to make sure Regina hears that little fantasy before she runs headfirst into a swarm of well-meaning mother-in-law opinions."

Margaux paused to giggle with Chelsea when Jade

stretched again and let out the most endearing miniature fart the world had ever known.

"No stink detected," Margaux said, "so I think we're still in clean diaper territory. Something you want to remember is most new parents have months to get ready for all of this, and it still knocks them for a loop. They more or less know the date when they'll hand over a huge chunk of their lives and their hearts. From what you've told me, you and Regina have been working on this for years, but it all happened all at once in the end. You've earned a little time to adjust."

"I wish we could have talked to you about it all, Auntie Go. We probably should have. After the first couple of adoptions didn't work out, we felt like... I don't know. Like it wouldn't be fair to put anyone else through all that rising and crashing hopes nonsense. Thank you for not being mad at me over that."

Margaux shook her head and wrinkled her nose at Chelsea.

"You two had every right keeping your business to yourselves, especially over something like this. My goodness, how could I be mad sitting here with you and your bewitching new daughter like this? Fair warning, she's already got me wrapped around her little pinky toe. I'll do anything she asks and be happy for the chance to spoil her."

Chelsea snorted. "I'm gonna call BS on that right now. You were always good to us, sure, and made sure we have fun when we were with you. But I don't remember you spoiling or breaking parental rules. Which I appreciate greatly now, by the way. I might have fussed about it back then."

At a murmured complaint and lips-pursed frown from Jade, Chelsea reached into the mammoth flower-and-glitter covered bag at her feet, extracting a pre-filled bottle.

"I mixed this one up as soon as we got here, so it should still be plenty fresh. I can get another one if you think that would be better." She paused when Margaux flashed her a mock-scowl. "Or, I could stop endlessly questioning myself, and we could both go with the fact that this one is perfectly fine."

She smiled and raised her eyebrows, clearly offering to take Jade.

And just as clearly happy to let Margaux have her chance at the delight of baby feeding time.

"It would be my pleasure to feed this little angel while I have the chance," Margaux said. "You'll have plenty of offers for help with that once the rest of the family gets here. I'm not afraid to admit I'm awfully glad to be the first. Think you might get a little sleep before they show up?"

Besides Regina arriving in the morning, several others would be making the trip to meet the new arrival. Including Chelsea's extremely proud and thrilled mother, who would certainly be claiming her new-grandmother time, as she should.

Chelsea tried her best to hide it, but the contortions of her eyes, nose, and mouth made her yawn almost as obvious as when she was a tired eight-year-old fighting going to sleep at Auntie Go's house.

"I might try to get a nap in if you truly don't mind. Once Jade gets her belly full, she usually goes right back to sleep for an hour or so. Then get ready for hard-core playtime."

She smoothed Jade's soft fluff of hair, then leaned her head against Margaux's shoulder for a few seconds.

"Honestly," Chelsea said, "I'm glad we get a little time here with just the three of us. I can't wait for everyone to meet her, but they can be a lot all together. Thank you so much for flying up on such short notice."

Jade clenched her fists just as her dewy soft cheeks turned red, and Margaux took the offered bottle.

"You are more than welcome, Chelsea. That's one of the

best things about being my own boss. I get to set the schedule. Don't ever hesitate to ask for help, from me or anyone else. That's what experienced aunties are here for, you know. And I wouldn't trade moments like this for anything in the world."

KARI KILGORE

AUTHOR OF THE WORRY TRAP AND AT THE HEART OF IT ALL

ONE SIMPLE WORD

For everyone who loves unconditionally

ONE SIMPLE WORD

STRANGE as the idea might seem to some, Bev Martin had always loved her therapist's office.

Dr. Morgan kept the space cozy and comfortable, for one thing. For some reason, Bev made a point of sitting in a different part of the room every time.

Curled up in a boxy, oversized midnight-blue chair almost big enough for two. Sprawled across a modern version of a beanbag, filled with body-hugging memory foam with a velvety pink cover. Feet up in a cheery rust-colored recliner, or even perched on an endlessly adjustable matte-black office chair.

Sometimes according to her mood, or whether a specific part of her middle-aged body ached that day.

A few years back, she chose depending on whether she wanted to sit close to her husband during their joint sessions or as far away as she could get. Thankfully they eventually ended up sitting side by side on a dreamy, overstuffed burgundy sofa.

What Bev suspected deep down inside was she moved around to give herself a different perspective.

Wasn't that the whole point of therapy, anyway?

That might be a great question for Dr. Morgan, but not today. Instead Bev simply waited in the big blue chair, sock feet tucked under a fuzzy peach blanket.

A black metal waterfall fountain decorated with a bunch of sparkling, colorful rocks bubbled away on a table beside her chair, adding soothing sound and a much-needed touch of humidity to the air.

The office décor offered an abundance of visual choices as well.

A narrow shelf lined top to bottom with books that ranged from thick, scholarly tomes about psychology and the brain to trendy self-help titles to two rows of the latest best-sellers. One shelf was stuffed full of children's books for younger clients, or parents with kids at home.

Another wall held big, blocky shelves full of all kinds of toys, and not all of them for the kiddies. Soft, fuzzy balls and stuffed animals waited alongside old-fashioned options from her 1970s and 80s childhood. Rubik's Cubes, faded plastic action figures, even a brick-red Merlin game that tragically didn't work anymore.

Bev's personal favorite was an original Slinky. She'd worked out her anxiety during more than one session by tilting the metal coils back and forth.

A clear bin full of toy cars, another with bunches of dolls in various styles of clothing. Hand-sized beanbags, and modern fidget spinners. A couple of bins overflowed with samples of fabric in all kinds of different colors and textures.

Dr. Morgan always said she wanted to keep whatever folks needed to keep their hands occupied so their minds could dig in and do the work.

She even had several photographs from all around their southern Illinois town tucked in among her diplomas and certifications, just to keep things interesting.

The best wall as far as Bev was concerned was actually a window, overlooking the forested lot stretching out behind the office. Right now the view featured a gorgeous early season snowfall, coating each trunk and branch of the oaks, poplars, and maples on one side. The contrast with the winter-bare canopies and darker parts of the trunks created an irresistible landscape she'd normally have to drag her gaze away from to pay attention to anything else.

Instead Bev glanced at her watch again, trying not to get annoyed as the wait stretched past ten minutes and officially into fifteen.

Not for Dr. Morgan that day, though sometimes other folks did run over and push things back. Nor for Bev's husband Rick, who'd occasionally managed to arrive late for the string of appointments that had not only saved but strengthened their marriage.

No, today Bev and Dr. Morgan both waited for her nephew Jody, who kept texting that he'd be right there.

At least the office was pleasantly warm, and the aroma of Bev's second mug of cinnamon-scented coffee soothed her senses while it kept her hands toasty.

Sitting in this room waiting to help someone else instead of herself did present a nice change of pace. But she still fretted to herself about what might be bothering Jody enough to arrange for this appointment and ask her to join him.

A request that had come by phone, along with hesitant words and a tear-trembly voice that had Bev's own eyes welling up.

She jumped when the door clicked open and Jody walked in, shoulders rounded forward and eyes on the hardwood floor. His normally shiny red hair hung lank around his cheeks, and she'd never seen him out in public in his overly casual slouch-around-at-home brown sweatpants and hoodie.

"Hey Jody," Bev said softly, not moving to get up. She put her cup down in case her hands started shaking. "How's it going?"

When he glanced up, nodded, and resumed his careful examination of his own scuffed tennis shoes, Bev did her best not to gasp or show her dismay on her face.

Jody seemed to have aged in the couple of weeks since she'd seen him. Rather than a smiling nineteen-year-old, she would swear she'd just caught sight of someone in their late thirties at least.

"Hey Aunt Bean. I'm here, anyway. Thanks for showing up."

He shuffled over to the sofa and folded down onto it, like someone cut his strings and he simply collapsed.

Bev's head and heart ached with trying to match up this miserable version of her sweet nephew with the giggling little boy who'd purposely called her Aunt Bean after watching old black and white reruns of *The Andy Griffith Show*. Jody's mispronunciation of Aunt Bea grew on everyone—including Bev—to the point that most of the family called her that now.

She hoped Jody in particular never stopped.

Before she could try to get him talking and figure out what was wrong, Dr. Morgan walked in and closed the door.

She paused at the tiny desk she kept in the corner as usual, rolling a dainty black office chair into the middle of the room. Her short gray hair was a close match to Bev's silver, and they both dressed in typical Midwest garb according to the weather. This time of year that meant jeans, long-sleeved shirts, sweaters, or even nicer versions of Jody's hoodie, all of it in neutral colors they could throw on without worrying about matching.

Dr. Morgan never used a notebook or laptop or even a

tablet, but she also never failed to remember everything that happened in the last several sessions. Or to know exactly what needed to happen next.

Just a few of the many reasons Bev thanked her lucky stars such a great therapist lived so close by in their tiny town an hour and a half from St. Louis.

"Sorry to keep you waiting," Dr. Morgan said, smoothly covering for Jody. "I've got a cancellation after this, so no worries about cutting us short. Either of you need anything?"

Both of them looked at Jody, who gave a slight shake of his head without even looking up this time. Bev locked gazes with Dr. Morgan, each of them with little frowns of worry.

"Okay, then we'll get started," Dr. Morgan said. "Jody, you want to lead us off, or do you want me to jump in?"

Jody's only response was to lace his fingers together in his lap, twisting his hands from side to side. Bev chewed the inside of her cheek to keep from gasping at the tattered state of his fingernails.

What had gone wrong? And more importantly, how had she missed it?

Most of all, she struggled with the urge to jump in and try to *fix* it.

Neither she nor Rick had ever wanted kids, grateful from the beginning that they both preferred dogs and cats. But they'd both been overjoyed with the arrival of this wonderful boy into their lives nearly twenty years ago, and the wonderful assortment of nieces and nephews who followed.

Jody's parents were great, but Bev knew her brother was often a bit puzzled by his son's constantly changing passions and exuberant moods. She'd always loved giving all of them a break from each other by taking Jody on adventures, even if that meant nothing more than going for a drive so he could chatter to his heart's content.

Right now, much as she wanted to try to help, she knew from all her experience letting her husband find his words that the best thing she could do for Jody was sit still, keep quiet, and wait.

Finally Jody's narrow shoulders slowly rose and fell.

"I'll try," he said, barely louder than the fountain. "That's what we're all here for, right? This was all my big idea. Even with my parents' insurance picking up the tab, I don't want to waste everybody's time."

He raised his head and looked into Bev's eyes, and his throat moved with several quick swallows. Between that and the rim of dejected red around his blue eyes, Bev had everything she could do to keep from walking over and giving him a big hug.

When he spoke again, his voice was stronger, but it broke like it had years ago when it was changing.

"Aunt Bean, I need to tell you something. It's not...easy to say. But I'm afraid if I don't tell someone...besides Dr. Morgan, I mean...someone who knows me...not that you don't, Dr. Morgan, but still. Family, I guess, but not my parents. Not yet. Anyway."

He opened his mouth, then blew out a breath, rubbing his palms against his thighs.

"I don't think I want... No, that's not right." Jody scooted back on the sofa, pushing himself upright and sitting up tall. The words tumbled over each other like the fountain's water falling over all those little rocks.

"Aunt Bean, I *know* I don't want to be a boy any more. I've known forever, at least it feels like it, but I couldn't talk about it. Well, I talked to Dr. Morgan, for a long time now, and that helped so much. But I need to tell you, too. Because I'm sure, I really am. I just don't fit this way, nothing fits. I'm not *supposed* to be a boy, and I want to do something about that. Okay?"

Bev froze, more surprised than she'd imagined possible.

She'd wondered in the back of her mind for years whether Jody might turn out to be gay, or at least bi. Not because of anything overt he'd ever said or done, or his choices of friends or occasional girlfriends.

It was just a sense she had, that he wasn't quite going to fit in with the standard-issue in their family or their very small town.

Turned out she wasn't wrong about that.

Instead of launching into a hundred reassurances or a thousand questions, or giving in to her earlier impulse to gather him up in a hug like she had when he was still in diapers, she reached over and touched his hand. It felt like ice under hers.

"Okay, hon. It means the whole world to me that you felt like you could tell me. Now go one step more and tell me what I can do to help you with that."

Jody stared at her, eyes wide, and Bev was certain he felt as immobile as she had just a few seconds ago.

Then his eyes overflowed the same way her heart did.

He turned his hand over and grabbed onto hers and squeezed tight.

"Just listening to me, you know? Just *hearing* me, and not laughing or scowling or, I don't know, puking about it, that's what I think I need the most right now."

"Then that's exactly what I'm going to do. You tell me whatever you want to. We already know you don't have any trouble talking my ear off, right? So you go right on ahead."

He bounced their hands on his leg several times, shaking his head, but a tentative smile broke through the storm of tears.

"I knew you'd understand. That I could trust you. I was sure of it. But it was still scary, like I was going to crack into a million pieces before I could get the words out. And now..."

He closed his eyes for a second, wiping at the tears on his cheek with his free hand. "I don't even know what I wanted to say next. I hope you remember, Dr. Morgan."

Bev almost jumped again, same way she had when Jody walked into the room.

Because she'd pretty much forgotten where they were and who else sat with them. She was honestly surprised to see the snowy landscape through the window, the shelf full of books, the cubes full of all those toys on the wall.

Dr. Morgan didn't seem nearly as surprised, or to even know or care how completely Bev had forgotten about her.

"Great work, Jody," she said, nodding. "I know how hard that was for you. I'd say you were right in choosing the first person you wanted to talk to. The most important thing you told me you want help with is speaking to your parents, remember?"

A little of Bev's joy that Jody trusted her so much floated away, but not exactly at the thought of talking to her brother and sister-in-law. She wouldn't dare say for sure, but she *thought* that would eventually turn out okay.

She hoped it would.

But after that, the reality of what Jody was up against loomed with the unpredictability of the oncoming Illinois winter. From the rest of the family, Jody's friends at college and in town.

Too much of the world still didn't understand, and didn't care to learn more.

And too many people chose cruelty over kindness.

If she could stop a single bit of that without getting in Jody's way, or keeping him from doing it for himself, she'd do whatever it took to make that happen.

"Of *course* I'll be there with you," she said, squeezing Jody's hand. "We can rehearse until you're sick to death of telling me, or until it's as easy as talking about how the temperature outside *really* wouldn't be bad without the wind. If you need more time than that, you can switch to how the summer heat would be just *fine* without the humidity."

Jody snorted and shook his head, but he didn't let go of her hand.

"Think you can help me and Aunt Bean with that, Dr. Morgan? So we don't end up babbling about the weather for the next six months?"

Dr. Morgan laughed under her breath and waved one hand toward Jody.

"Whatever the two of you need, you know that. We're both here and on your side. Bev, Jody and I have had lots of time for questions and answers and talking it over. Do you have anything you want to say or ask before we go on and do a little planning?"

Bev hesitated for a second, not sure where to start, but wanting to share something. At least some kind of support or encouragement at the beginning of what was going to be a difficult journey.

She had a bunch to learn about what Jody was facing, sure, and how to help as much as she could. But she'd known Jody since birth, and being an auntie was one of the most important things in her own life.

Stepping into uncharted territory or not, she was always and forever Aunt Bean.

Then she had it.

The first thing she could offer to smooth Jody's long road into a better future.

"All I want to say right now is I wonder if my wonderful niece has considered what a gift her parents gave her all those years ago. You won't even have to change your name, sweetheart, not unless you want to. Think how much trouble that will save you."

Jody's eyes crinkled up even as more tears spilled over,

and her radiant smile lit the whole room. She pulled Bev up and into a tight hug, whispering the same words over and over again.

"Thank you."

KARI KILGORE

AUTHOR OF THE WORRY TRAP AND SONGS IN THE MOUNTAIN

A Gentle Nudge
in the Right Direction

For everyone who listens
and offers that loving, gentle nudge

A GENTLE NUDGE IN THE
RIGHT DIRECTION

ON THE SURFACE, at street level, the wonderfully designed retirement neighborhood didn't look all that unusual to Beth Azen's eyes.

A quiet, tree-lined street, with gracious but cozy houses that could have been built a hundred years ago. Brick, a few stone, mostly wood siding painted in rich earth tones. A couple with two stories, but almost all one-level cottages.

Her favorites had always been the Craftsman bungalow styles, with generous porches, solid construction, and deep eaves for capturing every possible breeze during hot weather.

If this muggy Memorial Day weekend didn't qualify, Beth didn't want to get the full experience. Even coming from her not-exactly-chilly home in Nashville, an unusually warm Saturday afternoon in the nineties and dreadfully humid was more than enough.

The real crowds would show up on Sunday and especially Monday, all mad for a day of cookouts and family reunions with their older relatives, whether the family wanted to (or should) be reunited or not.

Right now Beth enjoyed the peace and quiet away from

her busy neighborhood and hectic life in the city. Birdsong and a distant lawnmower or two created a far more restful air than traffic, noisy neighbors, and too much going on at home and at work.

She didn't mind one bit that someone nearby had gotten an early start on the holiday cookout—possibly in the lush common area shared by all residents—even if her stomach reminded her that lunchtime drew increasingly near.

The companionable squeak of the porch swing created a pleasant counterpoint to the low voices around her on the porch. Beth's great-aunt Louella sat beside her on the swing, using her bare feet to push off the cheerful sky-blue rug on the floor. The sight of Auntie Lou's bright red toenails made Beth smile, same as when she was a little girl and Auntie Lou had a lot more brunette than silver in her hair.

Two women and a man around her great-aunt's age sat around the porch, in white metal rocking chairs and a glider. Like the swing, everything was accented by midnight-blue cushions covered with powder-blue stars that Beth happened to know glowed in the dark.

Auntie Lou had made the cushions along with her own forest-green wide culotte shorts and the sunflower-yellow blouse. She'd made many a colorful and unique outfit for Beth and her various cousins over the years, which Beth wished she still had now, even if they wouldn't fit her much taller, lankier adult frame.

Instead she settled for her own denim shorts and purple t-shirt. She had no excuse for her unpainted toenails in such company. She'd known very well making this trip home to the Appalachian Mountains in Virginia—and especially visiting her great-aunt's lovely house in Hidden Springs— required certain preparations.

But she'd let her own stress and worry and trying to keep up with her boyfriend Steve's intense social and work timetable keep her distracted until all she had time for was escaping into her car for the five-hour drive. Nothing but a stretch of interstate-highway solitude with her wonderful redbone hound Janie snoozing in the back seat.

A break from over-scheduling that Beth needed more than she wanted to admit.

Being the youngest on the porch by a good four decades was one reason Beth kept her mouth mostly shut and listened. The stories in this crowd never failed to be utterly fascinating, and the best ones were more than a touch fanciful.

Even Janie stayed quiet on her perch of dog-sized starry cushions by the swing, big brown eyes following Beth as Auntie Lou pushed them back and forth. Normally Janie would have crashed out sound asleep given the slightest chance.

Auntie Lou's unchangeable habit of sneaking her bits of gingersnap likely explained Janie's attentiveness. Beth had finally gotten her to compromise and mix proper dog biscuits in with the little bag of treats in her pocket, and Janie didn't seem to mind a bit.

Beth's unsettled and downright grumpy mood kept her from talking much, too. Instead she half-listened to the soft conversation, sipped perfectly tart and blessedly cool sweet tea from one of her great-aunt's metal cups, and stared out at the mountains in the distance.

Nashville had a lovely landscape to be sure, with plenty of green and rolling hills and ridges. But the much higher folds and contours and deep, wild valleys of these mountains were home.

A home Beth dearly missed, more than she wanted to think about.

She shook her head and looked up when the swing stopped, realizing everyone else had gotten to their feet. Even

Janie had her head up, and her long, bushy tail thumped against her cushion. Each one of Auntie Lou's guests gladly handed over a bit of cookie (or biscuit) and scratched those long, soft hound dog ears.

A quick round of goodbyes—with the usual discomfort of people who remembered her as a little girl while she had no clear recollection of them—and Beth settled back in with Auntie Lou and Janie.

"Sorry we took up so much of your visiting time," Auntie Lou said in her musical, rising and falling mountain accent. "Just sitting her jawing away 'bout things you couldn't care less about if you worked at it."

Beth touched her great-aunt's hand and was rewarded with a surprisingly strong squeeze.

"No, Auntie Lou, I'm the one who should be apologizing. I haven't exactly been good company for anyone lately. Even Janie's getting annoyed with me being so ornery and moody."

Auntie Lou gave the swing a good, solid push back, hard enough to get a loud *gronking* noise out of the chains holding it up. And a confused, ear-flapping head tilt out of Janie.

"Now that's a good bit of pure nonsense and you know it. I've known you since the day you squalled your way into this world, Elizabeth Michelle Azen, and I say your company has been some of the finest since that very second." She paused to take a long drink of her own tea. "Now, since all the other gossip and chatter has run its course, want to tell me what's so much on your mind? Or you planning to keep it to yourself 'til you get it all worked out?"

Beth took a long breath, rubbing the bridge of her nose with her metal-cup-cool fingertips, once again taking in the tempting aroma of someone's hamburgers and hotdogs grilling.

"I don't know if any of the yuck gumming up the works

in my mind lately is worth talking about," she said, stretching her winter-pale legs out. "Pretty typical mid-thirties nonsense, I'm sure."

"Lord honey, that was so long ago for me, I expect I'm not remembering all that much of it. I'd never pry into your personal business, you know that. Just as sure as you know I'll listen if you've got a need to talk."

"And I'd be lying if I said that didn't sound wonderful to me. I haven't exactly had a receptive audience back in Nashville, not for a while, anyway. And Mom and Dad, well, we hardly ever see things from the same page. They love me, I know that, and we get along well enough. But we never really have understood each other where it counts."

Auntie Lou grinned at Beth, her blue eyes sparkling. The same way Beth's nearly identical eyes *hadn't* in the mirror for a while now.

"You're about as different from my nephew and your mother as you could be and still be kin. That was never going to be an easy road for any of you. I daresay you turned out a lot more like *me* than anyone should have expected. Not that they could have done much of anything about it."

"All the better for me, and I truly do mean that. Okay, as long as you promise to let me know if you have something else you'd rather be doing. You don't have a nice root canal scheduled or something else pleasant that I'd be keeping you from?"

This time Auntie Lou smacked Beth on the knee.

"Even if I had the worst toothache of my life and yours put together, I'd want to listen to you talk instead. You and me both know nice as our phone chats are, that will never be the same as sitting here together. So you might as well get to talking."

"Okay then. This is probably going to sound like a jumbled mess, because that's how my thoughts are right now.

My life too, that's the trouble." Beth tried to gather her thoughts into some kind of coherent order for a couple of seconds, then gave up. The best she could do was hope to speak slow enough that her words didn't trip and fall over each other on the way out.

"I think I made a mistake moving to Nashville, Auntie Lou. I get farther away from happy every day, even though everything's going great. Looks that way, anyhow. But I feel trapped now, and I don't know what to do."

For what felt like an hour, nothing broke the quiet besides the faint whisper of the porch swing's chains and Janie's soft snoring.

"I might have a whole lot to say about that, Beth, but I think you have more to get off your chest before I do."

Beth stretched out one of her bare feet as the swing moved forward, brushing her toes over Janie's warm, furry side.

"I guess it made sense before I moved. It must have, you know? I'd hate to think I uprooted myself and Janie and changed our lives for no good reason. I have a great job, and I do like my house, and the neighborhood, more or less." She shivered. "I feel ungrateful even thinking all this, much less saying it out loud. No one *made* me do any of it. I decided to."

"No, not from what I remember you telling me before you left," Auntie Lou said, shaking her head. "You were plenty excited about the whole thing, and you sure do have a sweet little house. But you didn't decide to move all by your-self. You and Steve both had your reasons. What's got you so tore up now, hon? You've had a habit of making all kinds of big changes in your life ever since you were a tiny little thing."

Beth shrugged. "No, it's not just me, that's the problem. You met Steve when you visited, so you know he's a good guy. We moved for his career a lot more than mine. *All* for his job, to be honest. He loves that, and the house, and the city, and everything else there. I can't..."

She took a quick breath, forcing the teary sound out of her voice, trying to grab hold of the hot, heavy sensation in her chest before it could run away with her. "It wouldn't make sense to ask him to move away from all that. He worked so damn hard to get himself where he is."

Auntie Lou rummaged in the pocket of her culottes, and the crinkling of the little brown paper treat bag got Janie up in a second, tail wagging madly. Beth scratched Janie's head, feeling the muscles bunch and relax as she devoured a little bit of dark brown gingersnap, followed by pale dog biscuit.

She appreciated the chance to catch her breath and get her unruly emotions under control more than she could ever say.

"What have *you* been working hard for, Beth? Or maybe you might want to take a little bit of time and think on *why* you've been working so hard, and I don't mean at your job. What do *you* want?"

Beth stared out at the mountains again, at the bluish haze fuzzing out the riot of green.

Then her eyes blurred the view even more.

As she so often did, Auntie Lou had gone right to the heart of Beth's troubles.

Which happened to all fit pretty closely around her heart.

"I want Steve to be happy," she said, too quietly. "And I thought that might be with me. I think he *is* happy. With our relationship, I mean. He doesn't seem to have as much...restlessness as I do, maybe. I'm afraid he's found the place where he belongs."

Auntie Lou stopped pushing the swing, and it slowly came to a halt. She looked Beth right in the eyes.

"You're afraid? That sounds to me like a strange thing to be afraid of."

Beth laughed, but she knew it didn't cover up a thing. Not any more than her words had.

For herself or for her great-aunt.

"That's because I don't think that's what I'm really afraid of. I'm beginning to wonder if I wouldn't be happier there if *I* was with someone else. Or if he might not be happier anywhere with someone besides me."

With those words, what felt like a creaking dam holding back too much water inside Beth's chest took on a jagged crack across the middle. She managed not to cry, but the rush and flood of sadness, regret, and hovering sense of relief set up a powerful ache in her throat and jaws that got worse with every tidal wave.

"Your expression doesn't look to me like one a happy woman wears," Auntie Lou said. "Certainly not the look I know and love from you. Mind if I say something? It's okay if you don't, honest it is."

Beth leaned closer and touched her shoulder against Auntie Lou's, mindful of the scourge of arthritis that had taken up residence there.

"I don't mind at all, no matter what you say. If I was going to get upset at you for saying what you think, that's on me for opening my mouth. Of course I want to hear it."

Auntie Lou pushed the swing again a few times, then shifted one of the thick cushions against the arm so she could turn most of her body sideways on the seat. She watched Beth for several seconds.

"Why did you decide to go to Nashville? I don't mean what you think of right now when someone asks you, or what you probably told your mom and dad, much as I love them both. I mean the first thoughts you ever had about it all back when Steve first wanted to go."

Beth leaned forward and held her face in her hands for a second, not wanting to get into this after all.

A feeling that she knew meant she very much *needed* to keep talking while she had the chance.

Once she got herself through this visit and back to Nashville, back to home and routine and Steve and all that constant motion, she'd have a struggle getting the words together inside her own head. Months or years might pass before she managed to get them out into the world again.

She didn't even want to consider how hard and established the unhappiness inside might be by then. Maybe too hard and thick to break.

"I love him, of course." She squeezed her eyes closed and held her breath until her head thumped in time with her heart. Then she forced herself to look into Auntie Lou's eyes. "Or at least I thought I did. I'm not so sure about that now. But he's kind, and good with Janie, and he takes good care of the house and the yard. And me. He's got such a bright future ahead of him, you know?"

Auntie Lou smiled, but she was shaking her head.

"Did you notice no one is saying Steve *isn't* all of those things and maybe even more, honey? No one outside your own head? Now, I'll tell you what I noticed, and you can ignore every single word if you want to, you know that. When you talked about moving to Nashville, you talked about wanting Steve to be happy, remember? I didn't hear one thing about wanting *you* to be happy. That's not like the sweet Beth I know, to turn your back on what matters inside your own heart."

Beth looked down at her own hands, not all that surprised to see them knotted together in her lap so hard the skin was turning pale.

"That makes me sound almost selfish, doesn't it? Worrying so much about myself?"

"Now that right there sounds like your parents talking. They always mean the best for you, I'm not saying they don't. But from what I remember, you being set on finding your own path, even if that meant chopping and hacking out a brand new one to suit you, is one of the things they never quite seemed to make sense of."

She leaned forward again, but instead of moving toward the little treat bag for Janie, she stared right into Beth's eyes.

"Same thing with Steve's bright future, isn't that so? I never have forgotten that boy you dated right at the end of high school, remember? Real nice boy, kind and good like you said. Played baseball, wasn't it? Planned to go off to college for that, and to study some kind of business or such. Your mom and dad sure did love him, practically had you picking out your wedding china before graduation. But *you*, Beth? I knew the second I saw you two together that your heart never did even catch a spark, much less blaze up into a pure fire."

Beth couldn't stop a laugh from sneaking out, and the tear that scooted out at the same time felt less painful than she'd feared.

"Yeah, I remember Kenny. You saw things a heck of a lot more clearly than my parents did for sure. More than me for a while, too. He ended up doing real well for himself, living down in Atlanta with a wife and three kids last I heard."

"Exactly the life he wanted?"

"For at least as long as I knew him, yes. He wanted all the traditional stuff. The house in the suburbs and the steady job and a family. I wouldn't admit this to most people, and certainly not to Mom and Dad, but I'm not sure I want any of those things. Well, maybe I thought I did when I went with Steve, huh? Or maybe I thought I *should* want them."

Auntie Lou winked, and Beth couldn't resist rolling her eyes.

"Think you might be onto something there?" Auntie Lou dug into her bag of treats. She held up a pale dog biscuit so Beth could see before tossing it to Janie, who caught it without moving much besides her mouth.

"I don't have to remind you I had two wonderful husbands," she went on, "and neither one of them wanted children either. The honest truth is that freed us up to love on all you kids as much as we wanted to. I never felt for one single solitary minute like I didn't have a family, not even now."

Beth once again rubbed her toes through Janie's fur, getting a long, contented doggie sigh in return.

"I don't feel like that either. I've had one goofy sweet dog or another since I was nineteen years old. I'm sure they'd be surprised and pretty dang mad if they thought I didn't consider them family. Still..."

Auntie Lou squeezed Beth's shoulder.

"Were you planning to marry him, hon?"

Beth waved one hand in no particular direction, which felt entirely appropriate.

"I didn't... We hadn't... Neither one of us has much mentioned it, not even after a few years together. I guess that might be a sign. Either he's not the one, or I'm meant to be an old hound dog lady someday. That might not be too bad."

"Well, I'm not one of those folks who think people who love each other *have* to get married, not these days. But I do believe loving each other needs to be part of the bargain." She stopped pushing the swing, and kept quiet until it coasted to a gentle halt.

"This might sound like I'm changing the whole subject of the conversation, so let me ask you if you feel better than you did before."

Beth raised her eyebrows, taking a minute to truly consider the question.

"I still feel sad, and worried about what I'm going to do. Ending a relationship never is easy, even when it's ready to pass on out of the world. Moving is always a big hairy nightmare, too. But yeah, I do feel better, Auntie Lou. Like I can think and breathe again for the first time in a long while."

She leaned forward this time and hugged Auntie Lou, whispering, "Thank you."

"You're more than welcome, Beth, like you always are. I didn't do much besides give you the space to speak up. One thing I've learned in all my many years is sometimes that's all a body needs. What I was going to say before is I'm wondering how well you remember my own mother. Your great-grandmother Pearlie Johnson."

Beth watched a minivan stuffed full of people roll slowly by, probably arriving for the cookout she kept smelling.

"Not very much," she said. "Only things like how warm and soft she was, how good she smelled. I always felt safe with her. From what I've heard, she had kind of a unique outlook on the world."

Auntie Lou smiled and nodded. "That she sure did. When we were all growing up, we thought Mommy had the most wonderful imagination of anyone we knew. Always telling stories better than any of the picture books we had. I didn't understand until I was grown how much of what she told us seemed as real to her as we did. Thank goodness Daddy had already learned how to take care of us by the time she started having so much trouble, and other folks helped out, so we never wanted for much."

Beth hesitated, not sure what to say. Anyone her age or younger would worry about neglect in a case like that. But all of her relatives from that generation seemed okay, at least by the time she met them.

"I'm glad everything worked out for you all," she finally said.

"We did all right. What I'm wanting to tell you is I think some of the things Mommy saw and heard and maybe even dreamed about were the truth. She spoke of both of my husbands before I ever met them, same for my brothers and sisters. And she spoke of others in the family, too, over the years. All the way until *you* were born, Beth. You were the last one she got to hold before she passed away. No one else had a baby for several years after."

Chills ran along Beth's arms despite the heat.

"What did she say?"

"What I've always figured is folks shouldn't know too much about what's to come, and the rest of us who knew Mommy felt the same. Whatever afflicted her in her last years might very well have been because of what all she did know. But right now, you're in a place where I truly believe what she said can help you."

Auntie Lou patted Beth's hand.

"She said you're to have a great love in your life, honey. One to change your heart and soul. From the way you're feeling right now, that's not what you've got with Steve. Maybe that's exactly why you're so antsy with wanting to make a new start."

When Beth managed to breathe again, the tension she'd been holding in her shoulders and neck and back for what felt like months slowly melted away. The effect was as great and warm and deep as settling into a hot bubble bath after a day of shoveling snow in the freezing cold.

"You know what, Auntie Lou? I think you might be right. Just hearing you say that has me feeling better than I have for a long, long time."

"That does my own heart a world of good, Beth." She reached out and grasped Beth's hand, squeezing tight. "I know you'll find your way to the right decisions like you always do. And you and Janie will land exactly where you're supposed to."

Janie raised her head at the sound of her name, then held her nose high and sniffed for several seconds. She snorted out a big sneeze before grumbling and putting her head down again.

"I think we will, Auntie Lou. Especially if we can get some food into her always-empty hound dog belly. Is that cookout I smell for everyone, or just one house?"

Auntie Lou scooted around and stood, and Beth hoped she moved so well when she got to the same age.

"That one's for everyone, hound dogs included. Just let me get some shoes on and we'll walk over and see what we can't get into. I sure am glad we got a chance to talk."

Beth stood beside her, then leaned down for another good hug.

"Me too. Talking to you always sets my world right."

Beth stepped into her sandals as Auntie Lou went into the house, and a group of residents strolled by on the sidewalk. Likely on the way to that same wonderful aroma.

She retrieved Janie's leash, waiting for her to stop dancing in place long enough to kneel and snap it onto her collar.

"What do you think, Janie girl? Ready for another big change? I think it's about time we got ourselves back to these mountains."

Janie answered with an outburst of sweet kissies all around Beth's cheeks and chin, and a huge grin Beth couldn't help returning.

Between Janie, Auntie Lou, and her great-grandmother Pearlie, Beth finally felt ready to walk away from her current life.

And walk forward into her future.

KARI KILGORE

AUTHOR OF WINGS OF THE HEART AND TRUSTING THEIR MAGIC

The Foundation of His Past

A MISFORTUNE AND MAGIC STORY

For anyone who helps a kid get back to sleep

THE FOUNDATION OF
HIS PAST

By HIS SIXTH nearly sleepless night in the airhorse trainees' lodging house, Soren Cadwyst had a good idea of what was causing his problem.

But no trace of an idea of what to do about it.

Only the barest light from the banked fireplace showed the still and quiet forms of three other boys sound asleep nearby. The mixture of ordinary oak and a stunted, twisted tree that grew along the nearby coast created an agreeable spicy aroma along with a low, slow-burning warmth and light.

Each boy had a cozy, cave-like bed hewn into the stone walls, and everyone besides Soren seemed to fall into an immediate, deep sleep as soon as they crawled inside.

Sort of like the great ursine beasts he'd heard about in the Serthgluth Mountains surrounding the airhorse city of Maestar. If the rumors were to be believed, those huge, rumbling creatures took to their own caves or burrows as the weather turned cold, sleeping the months away until springtime.

Soren wasn't quite convinced the ursines existed, not yet.

A worried, increasingly homesick part of him suspected

the other rider trainees were making it up to make him look silly, or maybe point out how little he knew about his new home.

He sighed, rolled his eyes in the dimness, and turned himself to face the dark inside wall of his sleeping den.

The sheets and blankets were far heavier than anything he'd ever needed in his home in the massive coastal city of Casai, several days' airhorse flight to the south. The normally gentle Wrynath Sea protected the city from the worst heat of summer and deepest cold of winter.

Thank all the powers that be the sheets were soft rather than yet more torment for Soren's already tender skin.

Windy as Casai often was, the humid, gentle air was a soft caress compared to the chilly, constant gales blowing around Maestar.

Between that and taking every chance he got to get airborne with one of the magnificent airhorses, tucked in behind a far more experienced rider, his hide felt scrubbed raw.

The thick stone walls blocked out the noise of that never-ending wind, and his own little cubby brought even more peace and quiet. But he still caught the occasional grunt or snort from his housemates. All of them obviously exhausted from their hours of training, like he should be.

Like he *was*, honestly, in his body and heart and every part of him that begged for the oblivion of slumber.

Instead Soren shifted onto his back, trying not to focus on how tired he'd be once morning arrived. Or his growing certainty that he'd meet the dawn with precious little sleep yet again.

Not how he wanted to present himself when he and the rest of the new trainees met their stablemaster for the first time. Or when the day finally came to climb astride one of the incredible airhorses for his first solo flight.

His latest explanation to himself about his stubborn inability to drift off was missing the soothing rhythm of the sea's waves so far from home. The Diarthen Sea lay too far below Maestar to provide the same comfort, giving the city the protection of steep cliffs and towering city walls. Without that, Soren doubted anyone would be able to live there for long.

The waves crashed and pounded against those cliffs, and he sometimes saw spray and felt the mist against his face even so far up.

The sea voyage he'd taken from Casai to Maestar had proven a shocking and frightening lesson in just how fierce the vast bodies of water around the great continent of Hanferthen could be. Enough so he didn't particularly want to get too much closer to the rocky, moss-covered coast, without even a trace of sand.

He kicked the soft blankets off his legs, exposing feet that felt weary and pounded from long days in boots he wasn't quite used to yet. Made of leather in the same nondescript tan as all the trainees wore, they also sported a rigid metal toe to protect them all from heavy airhorse hooves.

Soren wasn't the only one who wondered if the beasts didn't aim for tender toes on purpose, especially the spirited yearlings.

No, even with the fire, the air in the room carried too much of a chill. Letting himself get too cold wasn't going to interrupt the stream of nonsense swirling around in his mind like the unpredictable currents in both water and air in this new place that hadn't yet grown familiar to him.

He flipped the blankets back into place, wondering if maybe he was hungry.

That could be it.

One of the endless refrains he'd already started hearing inside his own head was the exhortation to eat, eat, eat, but always feed the airhorses in your charge first! He couldn't deny his greatly increased appetite between all the activity and cold, fresh air.

Their first few days had been packed full of too many lectures and not enough time with the glorious, colorful airhorses that had drawn Soren and all the other young trainees to Maestar so strongly. A distressing number of hours mucking out stables for injured or retired beasts—often with their agitated riders nearby—didn't satisfy the way even a few minutes of grooming or inspecting the yearlings did.

One day, assuming Soren finally figured out how to sleep and made it that far in his training, he'd be paired with one of those yearlings. Then he'd begin his real training, learning how to stay steady in the broad leather saddle, to direct the amazing airhorses with his knees and feet and hands.

Finally shedding the same ordinary tan uniform that made him blend in with the rest of his training group until he felt sure he'd disappear, even if he was a couple of years older at seventeen and a few inches taller than most.

Taking on leather boots and woolen pants and jacket and helmet in the same shade as the airhorse he matched with. Vivid blue or green or orange, purple or copper or red.

Eventually winning his freedom to escape into the air whenever he pleased.

The dream that had taken hold when he was barely learning to walk and run on his own, if his parents were telling the truth of it. They'd disputed his wishes long and hard enough to make him not doubt a word they said about it.

Long enough that he'd arrived a few years older than everyone else.

Hard enough to make him wonder if he had a chance, if he belonged in such company at all.

Another shift, with a few kicks at the blankets and a vigorous re-fluff of his pillow for emphasis, and Soren once again faced out toward the room. Into the other sleeping berths, where shapes lay unmoving.

All except one.

Directly across from him, a pair of eyes gleamed in the soft firelight. Slow, deliberate blinks convinced him the boy was awake rather than dreaming with his eyes open.

Soren didn't quite understand why, but he closed his own eyes at once.

If he'd woken the other boy—his hazy, exhausted brain thought he was called Caldor—then the chances of him wanting to chat with Soren in the middle of the night were slim to none at all.

Immature and silly as pretending felt, it made more sense to Soren than an awkward and possibly annoyed conversation in the middle of the night.

Or worse, waking the other two boys so they could all be irritated at the gawky, shy, coastal boy together.

Soren already felt outcast and strange enough for being older, and so terribly inexperienced. Even with airhorses as occasional visitors during his life in Casai with a family full of stone and wood builders had hardly prepared him for the finer points of caring for airhorses.

Their delicate, furry wings, or their sturdy hooves, or their impressive teeth. How to fit and adjust the heavy leather saddles so they didn't chafe or bruise. The vital work of keeping them clean and making sure sweat didn't build up in their fur, especially under the saddle.

Neglecting that duty could get a trainee or even a fully experienced rider grounded in a hurry.

Soren kept his eyes squeezed closed when he heard the younger boy, Caldor, slowly push back his own covers and get out of bed. A few quick footsteps padding across the room, and the heavy wooden door squeaked open, then closed. Only did then Soren let out his breath.

The privy room down the hall was shared among several rooms full of boys, so that was a sensible reason to be up and about. Unlike the heartsore and homesick mental jumble that had Soren so wakeful.

At least until Caldor returned, he was alone with his thoughts, spinning and tangling and pulling him into a never-ending whirlwind when he truly did need rest more than he ever had in his life.

Before he could get himself even more twisted into his blankets and his head, the door opened again.

And in a single breath, annoying his roommates became the least of Soren's worries.

Caldor scurried back to his own bed with his head down, disappearing under a flurry of blankets without a sound.

And Tante Fodry stood alone beside the door, an enchanted candle with a sparkling silver flame lighting her angular, kind face.

Soren wouldn't possibly be courageous enough to ask, but he thought her age fell somewhere between his mother and his grandmother, even though she looked younger somehow. Her wavy red hair was always piled in a scattered bun on top of her head, where the Maestar wind could play and rearrange it at will.

Tonight she wore the typical robe for all the adults who attended to the lodging houses for younger trainees. Nowhere near as long or elaborately decorated as true Honored Mages, the women and men who wielded magic as easily as they breathed, and who Soren was more than halfway frightened of. This lavender robe had a lighter weight of wool than the Mages' robes did, and fell around Tante Fodry's knees rather than brushing the ground.

Her lively abundance of hair made it clear she rarely used the hood to shield her head from the wind.

And even with her perpetually friendly and under-standing expression, Soren tried to shrivel himself even more back into his sleeping nook, not wanting to face how he'd disrupted yet another person's evening.

Tante Fodry smiled then, and motioned him forward with her free hand, obviously wanting him to join her.

No matter how hard he tried, he couldn't quite figure out a way to pretend he was asleep now that she'd seen him.

The slightest breeze of hope that she might actually be able to help got him untangling the blankets and swinging his legs over the edge of the bed. He only stopped long enough to shove his feet into warm leather slippers, lined with dark green wool against the chill of the stone floor, and shrug into the flight jacket he hadn't yet had a chance to use in the air.

"Care to take a walk with me, Soren?" she whispered, leaning close enough that he smelled the pleasant floral aroma that lingered around her. "I find myself awake often this time of night as well."

Soren hoped the odd, pale light of the candle didn't show the blush he felt spreading from his cheeks and ears and even down his throat. He nodded and padded out of the silent room behind her.

The hall was nearly as dim as the sleeping room, lit only with a series of floor-level enchanted lights, adding a golden glow without risk of burns or careless trainees catching their pants or skirts on fire.

That had been one of the many surprises when Soren arrived less than a week ago: how much magic was a part of the daily life of the city of airhorses.

Full Honored Mages frequently traveled through on their

mysterious business, of course, as they did throughout all the lands as they were needed and as it pleased them.

But many people like Tante Fodry—with enough magical training to give them a substantial measure of power —lived and worked around airhorses, riders, and trainees alike.

She patted Soren's shoulder as they walked along the gentle curve of the hallway.

"I'm sorry I woke Caldor," Soren said in a low voice, more from embarrassment than worries of his voice carrying through the thick wooden doors to other sleeping rooms. "And I certainly didn't mean to interrupt your night, Tante."

She shook her head and smiled again.

"You didn't wake Caldor or interrupt me, Soren. I truly am up and wandering these halls during the night. And I asked Caldor a couple of days ago to let me know if you kept having trouble sleeping. He hadn't said a word to me about it before tonight."

"If it wasn't him, who told you? That I haven't been sleeping much, I mean."

As soon as the words life his mouth, Soren realized he'd just confessed whether he wanted to or not.

"No one *needed* to tell me," she said. "Anyone who pays attention would know you're exhausted most of the time. But the truth is I have my own ways of knowing how trainees are faring, Soren."

They walked for several more steps before Soren worked up the courage to say anything else.

"Is that with magic, Tante? The way you can tell?"

She nodded and tilted her head back and forth at the same time.

"I can tell by the shadows around your eyes, and the way you're shivering and cold all the time. And yes, one of the ways I watch over all of you is with magic. The adjustment of leaving home and traveling so far is a difficult one, even for people much older and more experienced than most trainees. My sworn and sacred duty is to make sure none of you come to harm because of it."

Soren held out both hands, then let them collapse to his sides.

"I *am* older than everyone else. But no one else is falling behind the way I am."

Tante Fodry came to a stop beside a boxy staircase that turned at sharp right angles going down to the ground floor and up to two more levels above. Every other step held a tiny, heatless blue candle that only cast light ankle-high.

"First of all, what makes you think you're falling behind? And have you ever considered that you may be struggling more *because* you're older than many of the others?"

A perpetually groggy, half-asleep part of Soren suspected he was being rude, but he couldn't seem to stop himself. He crossed his arms and shook his head, kicking at the floor. The soft slippers didn't make enough noise against the stone to make it worth the effort.

"I'm know I'm falling behind because I can't remember things. Nothing stays straight in my mind for more than a few seconds, and I used to be so *good* at that. I thought... Shouldn't being older make me better at learning, at figuring out how to feel like I actually belong here?"

"This may be hard for you to understand, or even to believe," Tante Fodry said. "But a simple lack of sleep can play havoc with every single thing inside your head. Memory, appetite, balance. Even whether you feel warm or cold. What if I told you that's one of the many reasons we don't let brand new trainees into the air for a few weeks? At least half of you are so sorely in need of rest that you'd fall off your mounts before you ever had a chance to get comfortable in the saddle."

Soren opened his mouth meaning to argue, but he wasn't sure what to argue about.

"There are others having the same kind of trouble?"

"Yes indeed," Tante Fodry said in a low voice. "More of you than not, and with every new group of trainees. No matter how deeply you dream of spending your life with our magnificent beasts, or how badly you wish to join us here in Maestar, leaving your home and family behind is no small matter. And how could you possibly know how it will affect you until you've done it?"

Soren shook his head and looked back toward his sleeping room. Where he was sure everyone else was oblivious to the world, and unaware of his own turmoil.

Even Caldor had probably dropped right back into sleep after delivering his news about Soren.

"The others in my room seem to fall asleep right away and never stir until the morning. I wish I didn't know that as well as I do. I don't know *them* very well at all, though. Making friends has never come easily to me like it does to most."

Tante Fodry nodded slowly, and her smile was sympathetic.

"You wondered why being older didn't help you figure out whether you belong here. The truth is you won't truly know if this is your place until you begin working with airhorses more directly. It has nothing at all to do with age. But the fact that the other boys in your room fall asleep more easily quite likely does. Perhaps you'd like to walk a bit further with me?"

Soren rubbed his face with his hands, fighting back all the conflicting voices in his mind that got so much worse at night. When everyone around him slumbered and the silence roared so loudly his ears rang with it.

"I'll walk with you, Tante. Otherwise I'm too much alone with my thoughts."

They started down the stairs, and the air seemed to grow warmer around them as they went.

"As far as making friends," she said, "that doesn't come easily to all of us, nor does it have to. The friends you do find will be loyal and true. Tell me, did you ever have trouble sleeping when you were younger? Two or three years ago, when you were the same age as the boys in your sleeping room?"

"Sometimes, when I had difficult days. Or when I was ill. But not very often. Not like I do now."

"What do you think changed?"

Soren concentrated on his footing as they reached the ground floor, where the last circular group of sleeping rooms waited in silence. Partly so he could try to work out how to answer what should have been a simple question.

But as Tante Fodry continued on, descending to a level he thought was forbidden to trainees, his mouth operated on its own.

"I guess I just worry more," he said. "No matter how hard I try to fall asleep, I can't seem to get my thoughts to stop. It got worse after I came here, even though I'm so tired all the time."

The steps here had what looked like a lighted rope along the bottom of each, glowing red like the coals of the banked fire in his room.

"I'm sorry to tell you that *is* part of getting older," Tante Fodry said. "Your mind learning how to roam free and drag you along with it, no matter how you might wish for darkness and silence inside your own head. That's one reason why this transition can be more difficult as trainees grow older."

Soren kept his fears about being *too* old to himself.

"What's the other reason?"

They stopped in front of a low arched door, with a rope of glowing violet following the curve across the top.

"Because you're old enough to understand what you've leaving. What you're giving up, and how much you'll miss it. Even in the face of reaching for something wonderful, you sacrifice what you've known your whole life long."

All the air left Soren's body in a rush, leaving him light-headed and dizzy, and his chest feeling like hot water flooded upward toward his throat.

He'd been so focused on convincing his parents to let him go—a multi-year battle he was sure he'd only won through his own sheer persistence—that he hadn't focused on how he felt about leaving them behind.

He dragged in a hitching breath, determined not to cry in front of Tante Fodry or anyone else no matter thick and heavy the sensations and vivid images of home grew in his mind.

Slow, fiery sunsets, with warm sea breezes lifting his hair as gently as it did the seagrass. His fingers and toes warm in soft sand, the taste of salt on his lips. The boisterous spring festival turning Casai into a wonderland of trader ships and visitors from distant lands, their looks and accents as strange and fascinating as their goods.

The solid, dependable love of his parents and brothers and sisters, never changing even though they couldn't under-stand how badly he'd wanted to leave them behind.

Somehow none of that had really taken hold in the days since he'd left, choosing a rough sea voyage rather than weeks of travel overland. Not the feelings of his departure, the depth and breadth of the change in his life.

Or perhaps that gut-level understanding had been chasing him since he arrived in Maestar, hovering close by.

Waiting for Soren to close his eyes for sleep, and deliver himself into its cruel embrace.

He jumped when Tante Fodry spoke quietly beside him, drawing his attention back to the hall they stood in, and the door outlined in violet.

"There's no shame in missing your home and family, Soren. I daresay everyone newly arrived here feels the same way at some point, at least for a little while. Most for a much longer stretch of time. But there are easier ways to move through your days than spending all of your nights fretting and wakeful."

He managed a smile, and for now, the quivering sadness remained safely inside.

"I believe I'd feel a lot better about it all if I could just sleep. Is that... Can you help me with that?"

Tante Fodry offered her kind smile and nodded once.

"I can give you the means to help yourself, perhaps. A way to allow yourself to finally relax and sleep, so you can figure out the rest as you're ready."

She rested the hand not holding the silvery candle on the huge brass handle set into the middle of the door. Soren didn't see anything move or change, but a ripple seemed to pass through him, one that left his skin tingling and all the hair on his arms standing on end. He tried to hide his shiver, but Tante Fodry raised her eyebrows.

"I simply removed the locking charm on the door. Nothing to worry about, and nothing that will affect you. It wouldn't do for trainees to wander into our private quarters or storerooms."

Soren had no idea what he was agreeing to, but he nodded as she stepped inside. After a steadying breath, he followed.

The room beyond was far too small for any sort of sleeping room or living space.

A pinkish glow gradually came up from overhead, revealing a space only a few paces across in either direction.

The stone walls were lined with metal and wooden shelves packed full of bolts of fabric, spools of different metal wires, woven grass baskets full of sparkling rocks and gemstones. Bundles of leaves and flowers hung from hooks on the low ceiling, in varying states from freshly gathered to looking dry enough to crumble.

The same tingle washed over Soren with every breath he took of air thick with herbal and floral scents.

A narrow waist-high bench sat against one wall, its surface covered with fabric packets about the size of Soren's hand, each wrapped in copper or silver or gold metallic wire.

He stepped closer, noticing each packet was wrapped in a different pattern.

"What are these, Tante?"

Tante Fodry ran light fingertips along the packets, brushing so lightly that none of them moved.

"They go by many names in different parts of Hanfer-then. I've always known them as *bildeh*. They take on different properties and powers much like they take on all those names. All depending on the desires and needs of the one who holds them. All you have to do is choose the one that fits your hand."

Soren's fingers stretched out of their own accord, but he resisted taking the step that would get the bildeh within his reach. He was afraid if he didn't take his chance to ask the question that plagued him now, he'd never find the courage again.

Perhaps in this one case, his lack of sleep (and the resulting lack of his usual shyness) would serve him well.

"Did you train with Honored Mages? Is that why you can work with magic?"

Tante Fodry folded her hands together and bowed her head for a brief second.

"Indeed I did, a long time ago when I had around the

same years as you. You'll learn much more about Honored Mages and Dirgelan in the course of your time in Maestar, as you'll often work closely with them. So I'll tell you that much like those who undertake training with airhorses and choose not to become riders, some who study in Dirgelan choose other paths as well. I am one of those."

Soren finally stepped forward, holding his own hand over the packets but making sure he didn't touch them. The draw to let his fingers explore them as Tante Fodry had was strong, and growing stronger.

"You decided to work with trainees here instead of becoming an Honored Mage?"

She laughed, the sound of it delicate and musical.

"I decided I didn't want the life of constant travel and study, and I realized my path would take another direction. Working with young people suited me, but I could have done that in Dirgelan or anywhere, really. Much like many who come here, my first sight of an airhorse captured my heart and decided my fate."

She nodded toward the bench covered with bildeh wrapped in fabric of many different textures and colors.

"It often helps to close your eyes the first time you choose a magical object. That removes the distraction of your vision and leaves you to sense the one that suits you best."

Soren smiled and did just that. He then decided to create another distraction and let his hand work without his mind attempting to guide the way as much as possible.

"I saw airhorses all my life," he said, his voice high and airy. "But not often up close. They're in Casai all the time, helping traders, collecting people traveling on the great trading ships. The sky is filled with them around our spring festival time, almost as much as it is above Maestar."

He let his hand drift, as if moving through the air with

the airhorses, catching the warm sea breezes so unlike the fierce winds around Maestar.

"For me," he went on, "it was the first time I stood face to face with an airhorse. I only had seven years, so the truth is I was staring up at her." The memory gradually floated out of the distant past in his mind, bringing itself into vivid reality all around him. "She was *gorgeous*, a sort of scarlet that I've never seen since. Her coat sparkled in the sunlight like it was woven out of some kind of metal or covered with gemstone dust."

Soren laughed to himself, only half-aware that Tante Fodry still waited quietly beside him.

"She had the strangest scent, like the warmth of a cooking fire. Her rider took the time to speak to me. He even let me stroke her chest and wing. From that second on, I couldn't imagine doing anything else once I grew up. I wish I could remember either of their names so I could let them know I'm here. Maybe say thank you."

His fingers brushed across the bildeh as he spoke, over textures scratchy and smooth, cold metal and warm fabric.

Then one hit him with tingles turned up high enough to bring explosive arcs of purple lightning above the Wrynath Sea into his mind.

He shifted his grip until it was safe in his hand, and he felt harder edges of something shifting inside a velvety soft cover.

Soren made sure to turn his face up before he opened his eyes, so he'd be looking at Tante Fodry rather than staring down at what he hoped was the bildeh he was meant to have.

She smiled and nodded, holding out both of her hands. His disappointment must have shown on his face.

"Don't worry, Soren, I have no intention of taking this from you or making you choose another. I only need to hold your hand in both of mine and help you complete the link between you and your bildeh."

He started to say he hadn't been worried, but fear of her somehow being able to read his mind as easily as she'd read his face kept him silent. He turned his hand palm up, with a loose grip on the bundle that already felt much warmer than when he first touched it.

Tante Fodry's grip was cool and strong, and covered all of Soren's hand and the bildeh within.

"If you wish later on," she said, "you may ask me or another of the tantes or even an Honored Mage to help you open this bildeh, so you can see what's inside. I'd suggest waiting until you're calm and secure in how it's used. Because the truth of a bildeh and many other magical objects is what the maker puts inside scarcely matters. It's what the holder, the *owner*, puts inside that creates the true power."

She gazed into his eyes for several seconds, and Soren was sure he saw sparks of purple lightning in her eyes. When she closed hers, he did the same.

"Soren Cadwyst, I give you leave and encouragement to fill this lifeless bildeh with the memories, the joy, the essence of your childhood. The foundation for your life no matter how far you venture, with airhorses or whatever your path proves to be. This bildeh can hold and protect your hopes, your dreams, your understanding of the things that matter to you most."

She squeezed his hands and let go. After a moment, Soren looked into her eyes.

The welcome he saw there felt like stepping into the warm sea after a lifetime trapped in a distant and foreign land.

"And when I've done this, Tante?" he said, filled with a confidence he couldn't explain but welcomed as if it was his next breath. "How will I know I've finished? That I've succeeded?"

"The fear of losing the core of yourself will depart, and I dearly hope your sleepless nights will mostly depart along with it. I'd never promise you complete or permanent success, with this or anything else in your life. Like many tasks that are the most worth doing, you may never finish. But I can tell you all these things will become more likely as your desire and your training align themselves with the reality you wish to dream into the world."

Soren gripped the bildeh in both of his own hands now, pressing carefully with each of his fingers in turn. More than the contours and shifting contents, he sensed rippling colors traveling up his arm and into his heart and mind with every touch and movement.

And he caught the strangest, most satisfying impression of all of his stress and worry and tension draining itself away into the bundle. Tucking itself into the empty spaces large and small inside for safe keeping rather than jamming into all of his waking and sleeping moments.

He didn't have to ask to know all of those things would still be there if he ever needed them. And that more room would always be available to him in the future as his concerns and problems turned into those of a grown man.

Then when the empty spaces were filled, a warm and loving current sparked into life. One that connected from Soren's fondly remembered past into his unknown but greatly desired future.

Firing whatever Tante Fodry had placed inside his bildeh into blazing, glorious life, opening the way for him to create the anchors he needed, the foundation for the rest of his days.

The work of building that foundation, of constructing it

piece by piece, experience by memory, hope by dream, would take much more than the rest of this night.

He expected the labor would stretch throughout the rest of his life.

But having the receptacle, the safe place, nearly brought him to his knees with relief and gratitude.

He didn't mind the tremble in his voice all that much when he spoke.

"I think I understand. But can I ask you a couple of things now? I'm sure I'll have more questions later."

Tante Fodry laughed again, and the sound was comforting rather than teasing.

"Of course, though I hope you'll answer one for me first. Why haven't you looked at your bildeh yet? That can only help you create your bond faster."

"I thought... At first I was afraid to, in case I didn't like the color or something that would sound just as childish saying it out loud. Then I was worried you'd tell me I'd chosen the wrong one, so I didn't want to get too attached."

She only held one hand out toward him.

When Soren finally looked, all he could do was grin like a happy little boy.

The bildeh seemed more like water than fabric in his hand—water that was a deep enough green to appear black. But the surface reflected more colors than his eye could catch. The silver wire holding it together was formed into swoops and curls that reminded him of the surf receding back into the sea.

He was almost certain he hadn't seen that one on the table before, though an empty space proved *something* had been there.

He decided asking if the bildeh formed itself to his desires could wait until later.

KARI KILGORE

"Where should I keep it? When I'm not working with it?"

Tante Fodry tilted her head, as if she was evaluating him, or perhaps whether to answer his question or not.

"Most airhorse riders, and others who have bildeh of their own, consider them private. So the main thing I'd suggest is keeping it where you can get to it, but curious minds won't be tempted. Or envious. Some keep them under their pillows when they sleep, or with their other private belongings. You'll decide whether to take it with you on your travels or leave it behind when the time comes. We keep bildeh for those riders who choose to leave them here."

"Do I need to make sure no one knows I have one?" Soren felt his cheeks heating at the arrogance of sounding like he thought he was special, but he still wanted to ask. "Is it something unusual, or secret?"

Tante Fodry raised one eyebrow. "Don't make the mistake of confusing secret and private. The truth is every rider trainee will eventually have a bildeh of their own. But we don't tell any of you about them until you need them. Until you're ready."

Soren closed his hands around the gorgeous green-black bundle and nodded. Being a couple of years older than almost everyone else in his training group, he knew very well what it meant to understand things people around him didn't.

And how to keep things private.

"I'll keep it to myself. I have no idea what to say, or how to thank you, Tante."

She clasped her hands against her chest and bowed for a second.

"Tell me whether you feel even a little bit better now, and don't pretend if that's not yet the case. And promise you will ask me or another tante questions when you have them. That's all the thanks I require."

Soren closed his eyes and slowly breathed in, asking himself the question.

Did he feel better?

Or at least feel like he *might*?

"I can't say I'm ready to go back to my room and fall fast asleep and be sure I'll never lay awake again. But my head feels less...full, I think. Less crowded and congested. Like more of the junk will drain away over time." He opened his eyes and nodded. "And I don't feel nearly so disconnected from everything, like I'm going to drift out to sea and get lost. I might be able to find my place whether it's here or not."

"Neither I nor anyone else could ask for more. Now let's get you back so you'll be in the right place if you decide to go to sleep after all."

Soren returned her quick hug, and a part of him that had been adrift and afraid finally settled itself into place.

Whether he belonged in Maestar or not—and he deeply hoped the city of airhorses would be his lifelong home—he at last felt sure he'd know the truth when he was ready.

And he'd hold the foundation of his past as he walked forward into his future.

ABOUT KARI

Kari Kilgore's wanderlust and imagination lead her all over the world on grand adventures. Her heart and family bring her home to her native Appalachian Mountains of Virginia. From that solid base, she and her husband Jason A. Adams bring those adventures to life in fiction.

Auntie Moon is her most treasured semi-secret identity.

Kari writes contemporary fiction, fantasy, mystery, romance, and science fiction, and she's happiest when she surprises herself. She lives at the end of a long dirt road in the middle of the woods with Jason, various house critters, and wildlife they're better off not knowing more about.

The Confidential Adventure Club

For Kari's exclusive free After The End stories and deleted scenes, discounts, early pre-sale releases, adorable pet photos, and a whole lot more not available anywhere else, join us in The Club.

Hope to see you there!

www.KariKilgore.com
www.SpiralPublishing.net
www.ConfidentialAdventureClub.com

bookbub.com/authors/kari-kilgore

amazon.com/author/karikilgore

goodreads.com/karikilgore

facebook.com/kari.kilgore.1

ALSO BY KARI KILGORE

I hope you enjoyed reading the stories in *Aunties Among Us* as much as I enjoyed writing them.

For more stories featuring fabulous aunties across the genres, drop by www.KariKilgore.com/Aunties. There are definitely more on the way!

For more stories where speculative elements are either slight or not there at all, head over to www.KariKilgore.com/ContemporaryFiction.

If you're craving more adventures from the Appalachian Mountains, and in many genres, swing by www.KariKilgore.com/TalesFromAppalachia.

For fantasy of many kinds, visit www.KariKilgore.com/Fantasy.

Be the first to know about release dates and check out more of my fiction, including almost every genre, at www.KariKilgore.com.

The Storms of Future Past Series:

Dreaming the Storm

Joining the Storm

Into the Storm

Fighting the Storm

Sensing the Storm: A Storms of Future Past Prequel

Storms of the Heart: A Storms of Future Past Romance

Storms of Future Past Books One through Four Collection

The Odd Society:

Independent by Means of Magic

Protected by Means of Magic

The Voices through Time Series:

Songs in the Mountain

Secrets in the Land

Walking the Ghosts: A Voices through Time Novella

Dispatches from the Galaxy Stories:

Restricted Species

The Becalmed

The Garbage Belt

Plurapod Pathogen

The Changes Cascade

Novels:

Until Death

The Dream Thief

Hand Me Downs

Protecting Her Own

Novellas:

Legacy of the Land

In the Pines

DNA Never Lies

The Box of Possibilities

Collections:

Fantastic Women: A Dark Fantasy Novella Trio

Fantastic Shorts: Volume 1

Near Future Forward (with Jason A. Adams)

Fantastic Shorts: Volume 2

Partners in Romance (with Jason A. Adams)

Dispatches from the Galaxy: A Space Opera Novella Trio

Fantastic Shorts: Volume 3

Escape into Romance: A Collection of Sweet Beginnings

Stepping Out of Reality: Short Spells of Appalachian Magic

Facing Down Extraordinary: A Series of Ordinary Heroes

Hacking Cybercrime: Dana Sanderson Short Mysteries

Shadows Mountain Deep (with Jason A. Adams)

Investigations Beyond Belief: The Initial Adventures of Deb Powers: Otherworldly PI

Passages in the Real World: Six Stories of Life's Transitions

Fantastic Side Trips: Side Characters Take Center Stage

A Kaleidoscope of Cat Tales: Five Stories of Cats and People Who Love Them

A Tapestry of Holiday Tales: Winter Adventures from the Odds and Endings Bookstore

Uncommon Holidays: A Different Side of the Season (with Jason A. Adams)

ADDITIONAL COPYRIGHT INFORMATION

www.ingramcontent.com/pod-product-compliance
Lightning Source LLC
Chambersburg PA
CBHW050422110726
47899CB00008B/2807